D1541611

THE HENLEY HIGH POETRY CLUB

CRUSHING

JUDE WARNE

EPIC
Escape

An Imprint of EPIC Press
EPICPRESS.COM

The Henley High Poetry Club
Crushing: Book #1

Written by Jude Warne

Published by EPIC Press™
PO Box 398166
Minneapolis, MN 55439

Cover design by Laura Mitchell
Images for cover art obtained from iStockPhoto.com
Edited by K. A. Rue

LIBRARY OF CONGRESS CATALOGING-IN-PUBLICATION DATA
Names: Warne, Jude, author.
Title: The Henley High Poetry Club / by Jude Warne.
Description: Minneapolis, MN : EPIC Press, 2018. | Series: Crushing
Summary: Hunter wants to be a writer when he grows up. When Wren, his dream girl, starts
    a poetry club, Hunter decides to push his creative chops to the max. But Hunter's longtime
    BFF Carmelita doesn't think Wren is for real. Hunter must decide between his dream girl
    and his best friend, and right and wrong.
Identifiers: LCCN 2016962594 | ISBN 9781680767155 (lib. bdg.) |
    ISBN 9781680767711 (ebook)
Subjects: LCSH: Poetry—Fiction. | High schools—Fiction. | Best friends—Fiction. |
    Interpersonal relations—Fiction. | Young adult fiction.
Classification: DDC [Fic]—dc23
LC record available at http://lccn.loc.gov/2016962594

For Warren, Gerry, Neil, Greil, and Jack

I headed straight for the back of the store, toward the Poetry Room, and grabbed a copy of Allen Ginsberg's *Howl* from its shelf. Carmelita was convinced that the line was, "I'm with you in Rockaway." A person had never been more wrong! I was disappointed in her.

"There—read the word for yourself! Right there."

She looked to see where the printed word "Rockland" met my index finger and rolled her eyes.

"Same difference."

"No, no, not at all! 'Rockaway' makes me think of Rockaway Beach in New York—'Rockland' is the name that Ginsberg gave to this mental hospital in the poem, where the poor schnook Carl Solomon was wrongly locked up."

Carmelita frowned. "Well, they're very similar words."

"Yeah, yeah."

Carmelita and I had been trying to test our recent memorization of the classic 1950s Beat poem. We had done well up until that line, when we had agreed to disagree, at least until I had demanded clarification. In poems, in literature, these things *mattered.* One word could make or break a writer's whole artistic point of view, the view that he presented to the world! I knew that this was true because I was a writer; so was Carmelita. Our pennames were Hunter Zivotovsky and Carmelita Lorca—which happened to be our real names too.

To solve the Rockland versus Rockaway riddle—a riddle that I already knew the answer to—I had dragged us away from our espressos at Caffe Trieste on Vallejo Street. We ran (much to

Carmelita's chagrin, through multiple yellow street-lights) down to one of San Francisco's many Beat Poet landmarks scattered throughout the North Beach area—the City Lights Bookstore. The Beat Poets were this super-hip group of guys who hung out in San Francisco during the 1950s; their writing seemed radical at the time and shocked a whole bunch of people then. They were romantic and enthusiastic about living and loving and just being alive. Their vibes still radiated into the twenty-first century, especially in their old hangouts—like Caffe Trieste and City Lights. My favorite was Jack Kerouac who had written my favorite book of all time, *On the Road*. The book was just about this guy and his friends traveling around America—but it was so much more than that.

On the Road introduced me to an attitude, an attitude that I truly wanted to steal for myself. It was one of coolness and intelligence, but it was also enthusiastic and life-hungry. It was immediate and instant and of-the-moment. It read like rock and roll music or something. One day, I hoped to write a book like that.

We momentarily abandoned our *Howl* efforts and prowled around the store. Section by section, shelf by shelf, writer by writer, book by book. We often prowled here; in fact, though we lived and high-schooled across the bridge in Berkeley, we were here in North Beach, and in this bookstore, once or twice a week. It was our second home. Carmelita and I thought that the more City Lights-ian oxygen we inhaled, the more artistic glory would make its way into our veins and stay there for all eternity. Maybe longer, even.

I picked up a copy of *The Rum Diary* by Hunter S. Thompson, my whacko-genius namesake, and toyed with the idea of purchasing it. I had read it before, twice, but didn't own a copy. Carmelita skimmed through F. Scott Fitzgerald's debut novel, *This Side of Paradise*. It was her favorite novel of all time. She was always a sucker for romance-infused self-discovery literature. I, on the other hand, went in for the more masculine stuff—as far as novels went, anyway—like seafaring adventure stories or Raymond Chandler's detective tales, tales that thrived on sarcastic, impossible-to-fool-for-long first-person narrators. You know, guys like me.

I put the Thompson book back on its shelf and motioned to Carmelita that it was time to split. Vesuvio Cafe, across the alleyway outside, was calling our names.

Whenever we went to Caffe Trieste or City Lights, we inevitably found ourselves at Vesuvio. It was the coolest establishment in San Francisco. We visited Vesuvio for the same reason we visited City Lights. We wanted our essences to mingle with those of writers who had spent hours and hours there, pondering and creating.

At Vesuvio, we ordered ginger ales and soaked up the atmosphere. We could only do this during off-hours, because technically patrons needed adult IDs to gain entry. So we usually went during the afternoons and hung out with the owner, Bobcat, one of my dad's best friends from college. Both Dad and Mom were professors who taught at UC Berkeley: Dad in Literature, Mom in Philosophy. The three of us lived together near the main campus in a book-littered apartment—we always had, as long as I'd been alive, anyway. Before I was born, Mom and Dad taught for a few years at Columbia University in New York, Jack Kerouac's alma mater.

Vesuvio could be called one of Jack's alma maters as well; when in San Francisco, Jack and his fellow Beat poets used to spend days there, sorting out the ideas of life, ideas that would go into their books. Carmelita and I usually did plenty of idea-sorting there ourselves.

We finished up our Canada Drys, waved farewell to Bobcat, and headed to the BART station to make our way home to Berkeley. We usually took the BART—or Bay Area Rapid Transit—to and from Berkeley and places in the main city. It was a Sunday night and I still had my Physics homework assignment to do. I dreaded it.

"This happens every weekend now, Hunter. I don't know why you always do your Science homework last. I do that first, because it's the worst—get it out of the way, you know? Then I have my Lit reading to do, and sometimes the weekly essay, last—the perfect way to transition from the weekend into Monday."

We hit the station, grabbed tickets from the machine, and waited for the seven-thirteen. The fog was rolling out and the October sunset hesitated in the open sky.

"That's because you're more logical than I am, always have been," I told Carmelita. "You believe in outlines too, before you start writing anything, don't you? Even though it differs slightly from the Beats' and my favorite policy of 'First Thought, Best Thought,' you probably get a lot more writing done than any of us ever have."

Hmmm. I thought I was onto something there.

"I guess there's a safety in not planning ahead with creative stuff, because without concrete plans, you don't feel bad if you never get them done," Carmelita added. "Once story ideas and chapter descriptions are written out though, there's, you know, a sort of obligation there. Obligation is motivating. It has to be."

Carmelita laughed loudly, flashing all of her teeth. I knew the sound of that laugh well but didn't always know what it meant.

"What's so funny, Car?"

"We're getting way too serious. Obligations? We like writing because it's fun, right? Fun is our motivation. The end."

Carmelita and I had been friends since the third grade, when we got into an argument over which Roald Dahl book was more awesome. I argued (and still do) for *The BFG*, while Carmelita argued (and still does) for *Matilda*. Every four or five months we revisited the argument for old times' sake, and to see if either one of us could finally convince the other that she was so, so, very completely and entirely incorrect. So far, original positions had held strong.

As we glided along the tracks, Carmelita put her head on my shoulder and closed her eyes. In middle school this would have been a forbidden and unwanted move in our friendship. But in recent months, physical closeness had grown kind of commonplace for us. On the train, walking down the hallways at our school Henley High, sitting across from each other at Caffe Trieste, Carmelita would grab my arm as she finished a thought, for emphasis perhaps—or something more. One time she had even held my hand as we walked to the Castro Movie Theater during the Silent Film Festival last June. Through middle school, neither one of us had ever become involved with anyone else; I felt that we had silently agreed to prefer good books to most real people.

Freshman year at Henley High, Carmelita was head-over-heels for her math tutor, Walter, and they dated for a while, but I knew it wouldn't last. He was an okay guy, but too mathematical for Car; he had no romance in him. The second he got accepted to Stanford—he was a senior then—he dropped Carmelita flat. Around that same time, I was almost in love with this French exchange student, Mara, who was then staying next door to my family's apartment.

The night that Car and Walter broke up, I decided to go to Mara and confess my undying love for her. I lay on the tiled hallway floor reading E.E. Cummings poems at Mara's door, and just when I heard Mara slowly opening the latch to let me in, Carmelita came running down the stairs from her place and over toward me, her face covered in tears. I took Carmelita back to my room, where she told me everything that had gone down with Walter. Seeing her weep like that really tore me up inside; I had never seen Car that sad. I held her in my arms as she talked and we eventually fell asleep on opposite sides of my bed, waking up the next morning to my mom rapping on the door yelling to get the heck up and ready for school. Carmelita snuck out while my mom was in the kitchen. Neither of us had spoken about that night since.

But that had been two years ago; we were juniors now and Carmelita's and my friendship was very status quo.

The train finally pulled into the Berkeley stop. Carmelita and I sauntered off toward our apartment complex. We lived in the same one, right off University Avenue—Carmelita on the top floor and me on the second. Car furrowed her brow and took my arm.

"What do you think Ms. Reese is going to announce tomorrow? Something big, I think."

Ms. Reese was our Lit teacher at school, and I had totally forgotten that on Friday afternoon she had made an announcement to the class—that another announcement, a big one, an exciting one, was going to be made during Monday's class. Carmelita continued to ponder.

"You don't think that she was half-joking, and

it's another *research* paper, right? I couldn't handle another one of those."

"Nope, Ms. Reese isn't the type to joke around like that. No, I'm hoping it's a field trip to Muir Woods again."

Carmelita poked me in the ribs teasingly. "You really go in for that nature stuff, don't you?"

"I do. I get much of my artistic inspiration from tall trees. So did Jack; ever read *The Dharma Bums?*"

"You *know* I haven't. And don't you ever think that maybe Mr. Jack Kerouac—or his ghost, really, given that he's been dead for decades—might get insulted if he knew you consistently referred to him by his first name only?"

"No, because he wouldn't, him of all people—of all *ghosts*. He was a pro-human free spirit."

We had reached our building. It looked like its usual open-airy California apartment-complex self. Ramon and Amelia, a new professor couple who had moved in just this year, were coming down the stairs. Ramon was in Dad's department at the university and Dad liked him, believing his research on Robert Louis Stevenson to be promising and an asset to the department. Dad was hoping to be appointed Department Chair soon; a new paper of his had just been published in a major journal and he was garnering plenty of industry fame, *New York Times* reporters calling him up left and right for quotes, you know, the whole bit. I liked Amelia. She looked like a young Joni Mitchell and had an intense love of Hunter S. Thompson akin to my own. She had lent me one of his *Fear and Loathing* books last month and I still had it in my possession, though I had long since finished it. I liked the way the book's pages smelled, the same gardenia scent that Amelia exuded as well.

"Hey Hunter, Carmelita!" Ramon greeted us. Amelia grinned and gave a half wave when they walked past us.

As Carmelita and I approached my apartment's landing, she snickered.

"What?"

"So when are you gonna ask her out? And don't you think Ramon'll mind that you're super-into his wife?"

"Cut it out Carmelita, I can't imagine what you mean."

"Oh stop, you actually blush in her presence. On a continual basis."

"I said cut it out." We'd arrived at my door.

"All right. Well, see you tomorrow morning then."

She reached up and kissed me on the cheek before continuing up the stairs to her apartment. She had been doing this more and more lately. It was a friendly enough habit, but I couldn't help wondering what it meant. I couldn't help wondering whether I liked it or not.

I walked in through the front door of the apartment to living room stillness, which for a Sunday night could mean only one thing: Mom and Dad were in the study at the end of the hall working on their respective class grading. I paused for a moment to listen and my ears soon detected the telltale paper-ruffling and Shostakovich record playing softly on Dad's old turntable. This was the apartment's standard grading audio that I had been exposed to since birth. It occurred every midterm and final exam season in each semester. It usually meant that the 'rents would be hard at work, and steadily so, for the next week.

I knocked lightly on the study door, then let myself in. As expected, Mom and Dad sat there in their favorite armchairs surrounded by papers.

"Hey guys, just wanted to let you know that I'm home. I'll be working on an essay in my room—and of course, have a *blast* with your grading."

"That's great, Hunter," Dad said without even looking up. "Thank you. Good to see you."

Mom at least put her papers to the side when she spoke. "Hi, sweetie, how was your afternoon? How is Carmelita doing?"

Mom had always loved Carmelita and frequently made vaguely obvious hints that I would do well to enter into a romantic relationship with her. She said that my absentminded intensity would be well-complemented by Carmelita's tell-it-like-it-is-ness. Mom was right about that, I guessed, and it was partly why Car and I were such great friends. As for the romantic stuff, well, I wasn't too sure. It would be a big leap to make from where we were now to anything like that. I pushed the thought from my mind.

"She's fine, Mom. We just bummed around North Beach for a while. Went to City Lights."

Suddenly and simultaneously, Mom and Dad both seemed to remember something and put their total focus on me.

"Hey that reminds me, Hunter, we ran into your English teacher, Sienna—Ms. Reese—earlier—" my dad began.

"—and she was telling us about the new poetry club that she's organizing at the high school," Mom finished.

This news of a poetry club intrigued me, and I thought that it might have something to do with Ms. Reese's big announcement set for tomorrow. I waltzed into the kitchen, grabbed a Coke from the fridge and returned to inquire further.

"What kind of poetry club?"

"Oh you know, a sort of after-school thing for students interested in writing their own poetry.

Sienna said the meetings would take place at Caffe Trieste on Vallejo, in the city. Sounded right up your alley, Hunter," Mom explained.

Dad continued, "It sounded pretty serious too, with auditions."

This seemed a bit ridiculous. "Auditions? Really?"

"Yeah, well, some sort of an approval process for entry or something. That Cooper girl, you know, Sam's daughter? Sienna said she's involved, that she's the student leader of it. Maybe you can ask her about it tomorrow."

"The Cooper girl? You mean Wren?"

"Yes, I thought it was an avian name. Yes, that's her."

All of my blood rushed to my head at the mention of Wren. I couldn't believe what I was hearing. I needed to go somewhere and think; a quick exit was in order.

"Sounds good. Well, I have to go work on Physics, and that essay due tomorrow and all."

Mom and Dad had resumed tunnel vision focus on their grading.

"Mm-hmm okay. Get to work honey. We'll be right here," Mom uttered.

"Good luck, Hunter," added Dad.

I walked with my Coke to my room, which was up the half-set of stairs at the other end of the apartment. It looked just as I had left it—in complete and total disarray. The Kurt Vonnegut short story that I had been reading was half-open on my unmade bed, and Sal my Siamese cat lay snoozing over its pages. He opened one eye as he heard me come in and rose to greet me. Sal was more dog than cat and was as trusty a sidekick as there ever was. He was a handsome devil too, with big blue eyes, shiny fur, and an undeniable masculine strength. We understood each other. I scratched Sal's neck until he lay down again and resumed his nap.

My favorite part of my bedroom's layout was the small French balcony that one of my windows opened onto. The bay breezes came rolling in at night and I would inhale them, imagining that I was inhaling the secrets of art, philosophy, love, and greatness. I hoped that it was working.

I took my soda out onto the balcony, admired the view of greenery below and sky above, and thought.

Mom and Dad's news was a lot to take in all at once. Firstly, this poetry club. I had been looking for something like this for a long time, and it hadn't existed—until now. I felt that I was a good writer, and I was getting better even, according to Ms. Reese. I consistently received good marks on written assignments, particularly the creative ones. In freshman year, Ms. Singleton had even taken me aside after I read aloud my story called "The Fourth Gun" to tell me that I "had a voice"—a powerful creative voice in my writing, she meant. I couldn't *stop* writing then, even outside of class assignments—short story after short story—and I had even tried my hand at a novella (current status: temporarily cast aside due to length requirements).

But by writing like a madman, I became an even better writer. And that was what I wanted to be. I wanted to get psyched up about the writer's life, the artist's life. To know what I wanted to do for the rest of my life felt pretty cool. But it also made doing some other things—things that were required of a high school junior in the United States such as myself—a bit annoying. SAT practice tests, for one thing.

One of the best aspects of being a writer was this: no experience, however mind-numbingly tedious, was ever wasted on me. Every event that occurred, every feeling that I felt, were all potential material for my future stories, my future books.

Now despite this history of praise—you know, of my "writerliness"—I was relatively inexperienced in writing any sort of poetry, especially the kind that I wanted to write (basically Bruce Springsteen lyrics without the musical accompaniment.) And the idea of a "club" with auditions suggested exclusivity to me—which still could be okay, if not for the involvement of Wren Cooper. If there was any one person in the universe in front of whom I did not want to embarrass myself, it was her.

Wren had moved to Berkeley from Los Angeles halfway through sophomore year. She lived with her dad, a music professor who had been transferred here from UCLA. I had never met Wren's dad but he was known by the Berkeley crowd as a post-hippie genius; he had apparently dated singer-songwriter Carly Simon during the mid-80s. Carly was one of the great loves of my life too, so I automatically assumed that he was a cool guy even though I had never met him. Mom and Dad had run into him once or twice at faculty parties but would never divulge much information about him when I asked—only that he was entertaining and told great stories.

It made sense then that Wren would be this way too, and she was, but with an added lightness. She was a nature girl, frequently wearing magnolia blossoms in her ebony-colored curly hair, even when they were out of season. She had a smile that was so incredible it made me borderline uncomfortable. This reaction was quite out of character for me. I was usually, even around ladies of high interest, a paragon of coolness.

Not with Wren. She did this thing where she turned my brain into a useless blob. And my brain was one of my favorite body parts so it really was a shame.

Physically speaking, I was tall—so tall that I had to hunch over to use the Henley High gym showers, which resulted in occasional and annoying neck aches. My hair was dirty blonde and long enough to hit my shoulders; I could almost tie it into a ponytail now. I wore thick-rimmed glasses due to my near blindness without them, and I wore the same lace-up utility boots that musician Neil Young basically lived in during the 70s. I knew this because

Wren had told it to me last month. It was our first authentic exchange with just the two of us involved.

I had first seen Wren coming out of Cal's Doe library the day before she started at Henley High. It was like a moment from a film, a slow-motion moment, in which the protagonist—that's me— experiences a turning point in his own life that will alter the course of his future. There was even music playing from a nearby food truck: "Sugar Magnolia" by the Grateful Dead. This classic song would always remind me of Wren but I didn't care; the moment was classic too.

It was a sunny and cool Tuesday afternoon in March and I saw Wren as I was leaving through the library's front doors. I had rushed there after class at three thirty to find a copy of Jules Verne's *20,000 Leagues Under the Sea*, the best adventure story ever written. The short story that I had been working on then was an underwater version of *The Swiss Family Robinson*, where this mer-people family was travel- ing through the Pacific on an underwater vehicle and it ended up crashing into a coral reef. The family had to reestablish its life in this new uninhabited part of the ocean, and antics ensued. Since this kind of event had never happened to me personally, research had most definitely been in order.

The main library at Cal had a much better selection of texts than the regular public libraries in Berkeley and was accessible to anyone, so it was usually where I borrowed my books from. The UC Berkeley campus truly was my second home. I loved its rolling green hills and many tan-colored buildings, each housing different academic departments. They were physical representations of knowledge found and yet to be found, and nerd that I was, they'd always inspired me. I'd been inside most of the buildings at one time or another with my parents over the years. I definitely wanted to go to college there when the time came, majoring in English, with a minor in Creative Writing.

So, on this afternoon last March, I had been leaving the library with the Jules Verne book under my arm, all set to take it out to my French balcony with Sal on his favorite red leash. This had been until I ran into Wren—literally.

I had momentarily looked over my shoulder to take a last glance at the library's roof, the most beautiful part of its structure. The next thing I knew I was tripping over the steps and falling flat on my face, my book flying several yards in the air. I was ready to tell the idiot who I had bumped into a thing or two when I looked up into the face of perfection: Wren's hazel eyes and wide smile and her outstretched hand to help me up. I took it and got to my feet as she apologized.

"I'm so sorry, man, I did *not* see you!" she said. "I was distracted by the truly beautiful architecture of this building. We just moved here yesterday and I'm giving myself a tour of the campus. Are you all right?"

It had been difficult to respond. Firstly, I was in pain. Secondly, I was spellbound by this girl. She continued to talk because I couldn't.

"My name is Wren, Wren Cooper. My dad is Professor Cooper in the Music department. He just transferred from UCLA." She paused and eyed me nervously. "Are you sure you're all right?"

I pulled myself together and reassumed my natural air of coolness.

"Yeah, I'm fine. It's fine. My name's Hunter. Welcome to Berkeley. I always liked that roof too."

Was that a *great* response or what? I put on my shades, smiled slightly, and strutted off à la Steve McQueen, star of my favorite film *The Great Escape*. I wished that I could've looked back to see if she was still looking at me, but it would have ruined the effect.

After that I didn't see her for a month. Then, one afternoon in mid-April, I saw Wren again in the hall at school. She recognized me and said hello. I asked her how she liked Henley High so far. I hadn't realized that she even went there; since we met I hadn't seen Wren and had assumed that she was a freshman at the university.

"I like it fine. Everyone's ultra-cool and friendly here. I really dig Ms. Reese's class."

"I have her, too. You're in the second period class?"

"Yeah, but next year I have it first."

"Me too. You like Lit, then?"

"Oh yeah. I love writing, poetry especially. Do you write at all?"

"Yeah, I do—short stories mostly. Heard of Vonnegut?"

"He wrote sci-fi, *Slaughterhouse Five*, right?"

"Yep. He's my main man."

"I'll have to read some of his stuff soon. Hey—I figured out who you reminded me of! Wow, it's been bothering me since we met," she said.

Wry smile, raised eyebrow, the whole bit. I was intrigued by the idea that she had been thinking about me since then. I had been thinking about her, too.

"Oh yeah? Who might that be?" Such sexy

dialogue had never before been spoken! I was batting a thousand so far.

Wren smiled. "Neil Young."

This momentarily took the sexiness wind out of my sails. I loved Neil, I loved Crosby, Stills and Nash, all those 1960s rock groups—but this was not what I had been expecting. I was pretty sure that Neil was in his seventies by now.

"*What?*"

"Yeah. When he was younger, of course. You walk just like him. And you have the same shoes. My dad's always watching old concert footage of him, so I know. Your hair's not long enough though."

She reached up and touched my hair, pushing it away from my face. It felt *amazing*. Wren smiled and started to continue down the hall. She paused and looked back at me for a moment.

"You know something? You're cuter than Neil was."

As she smiled and walked away I had to sit down

to regain my composure, cross-legged, right in the middle of the hall. I was lucky it was mid-period, otherwise I would've been trampled by flocks of Henley kids. What an awful way to go.

This fall semester we were in the same Lit class, so I saw Wren every day. We usually didn't get to talk much, only sometimes before or after class for a second or two, because Lit was first period and Wren was always late. It didn't help that I had to rush out at the end of every Lit class because my second period was Health, in another building all the way across the lawn.

Now there was an actual chance to spend some quality time with Wren, assuming that I could pass whatever kind of audition process was involved in this poetry club of hers.

I walked back in from the balcony and closed its door. Sal had awoken again and lay biting the pages of my Vonnegut story lazily. I picked him up and put him on my shoulders—one of our favorite and most-loved-by-crowds routines. He purred loudly as I paced the room, thinking.

My Physics homework still needed to be done. The essay for Ms. Reese's Lit class was due tomorrow—in approximately twelve hours—and thus needed my immediate attention. But all I could think about was the poem I was going to write, the one that was going to get me into the poetry club. The one that would make Wren see how I was the only man for her. It had to be masculine, meaning it had to emphasize *do-the-right-thing*-ness and express confidence at the same time. It had to be tough, cool, slick. It had to be seductive. It had to incorporate all the wisdom in the world—my knowledge of art, my grasp of history, my prowess in literary style.

It had to be the best poem ever written.

Sal jumped down from my shoulders and I opened my bedroom door to let him out into the apartment. Most likely he was heading to nose around the study, after noshing on a midnight snack from the organic, super healthy, longevity-boosting and intelligence-increasing dry cat food that Mom kept in constant supply. As if Sal's intelligence could possibly be increased. He was the brainiest Siamese cat that I had ever come across. I swore that he could even read.

I could still hear Mom and Dad's records playing on the turntable. They had abandoned Shostakovich and switched to Borodin's string quartets. I decided to leave my door open and let the aural inspiration drift into my room, too.

It was eight thirty on a Sunday night and I had an essay to write that was due the next day. I had to get into that poetry club. My fates as a literary legend and the future boyfriend of Wren hung in the balance.

I had some major tasks ahead of me, including that stupid Physics homework.

I was having the most awesome dream of all time when my alarm clock went off. In the dream, I had been sharing ginger ales with Dean Moriarty and Sal Paradise at Vesuvio. Sal (Sal the cat's namesake) and Dean were the main characters in Jack Kerouac's book *On the Road*.

It was seven o'clock on Monday morning and I had stayed up way too late the night before, till nearly one o'clock, finishing that essay for Ms. Reese. I shut the alarm off and reached for my glasses. I had to leave in half an hour if I wanted to make it to first period on time.

A shower, teeth brushing, and toast-and-coffee later, I was out the door. Before I left I was sure to grab my favorite jacket from the hall closet, the green army one that I had snagged for three bucks at a vintage store in Oakland last year. I ran down the complex steps into the morning chill and stretched out on the dew-grazed lawn to await Carmelita. It was seven-thirty and I was right on time. If things went as they usually did on Monday mornings, she would be five minutes late. I decided that I would take advantage of this and look over my essay for Ms. Reese's class to take note of any necessary last-minute edits—though obviously I didn't believe in edits, not really.

I believed that every draft was a final one, a belief that I debated tirelessly with Ms. Reese. As a high school Literature and Composition teacher, she believed the opposite—that the writing process was made better by drafts and more drafts, brainstorming sessions, peer-review groups, and read-alouds. I had accepted long ago that to succeed as a student and a writer at Henley High, I would have to jump onboard with the department philosophy and partake in all these rules-and-regulations antics. So I did, but I didn't enjoy it. First thought, best thought, like the Beats, was the only true way for me.

The work I had done the previous night read just as well this morning; I was pleased. Henley High operated on a routine daily schedule, and Ms. Reese's eleventh grade Honors class met during first period. Junior year English was devoted entirely to intense analysis of American Literature's greatest hits, my favorite bunch of novels and plays. Given that it was only mid-October and Ms. Reese's syllabus traversed chronologically, we were only up to Nathaniel Hawthorne's *The Scarlet Letter*. But I consistently pined for twentieth century authors—F. Scott Fitzgerald, Edith Wharton, John Steinbeck, Henry Miller, James Baldwin, Flannery O'Connor, Tennessee Williams, Zora Neale Hurston—all of whom would make appearances during the second semester. Despite this preference for more modern stuff, I felt that I had done a stellar job on last night's essay, the focus of which had been the risks of societal conformity in Puritan life. Should it be read aloud today in class, it would receive a standing O.

Suddenly Carmelita was there. She descended the complex stairs in a blue jean skirt, red flannel shirt, and sneakers, topped off by her reflective aviator shades. Car's signature red down vest dangled from her right hand, her Allen Ginsberg tote bag, full of schoolwork, from her left. As she came forward to meet me, my gaze landed on a morning sunray where it hit her bare leg. More and more lately I had been noticing the girled-out elements of Carmelita. As she drew in closer she caught my eye, stopped abruptly, and frowned, hand on hip.

"What are you staring at, Ziv? We are later than *late* this morning, yet you prefer to lie in the grass and ogle gorgeous girls as they walk by?"

I felt my cheeks flush a bright red. Man, I really

had to work on controlling that reaction! My cooler-than-thou rep at Henley High—a rep that came naturally but had most definitely been consciously promoted by me since freshman year—could and would *not* be taken from me. *Carmelita, why couldn't you stay as you were, as you had been?* It felt like elements of our life scene were changing and I didn't like it. I wished she would stop wearing that skirt at least; it would make it easier for me to stay friends with her. Just friends.

I stood up, stuffed my essay into my bag, and started walking in the direction of school. I trusted that Carmelita would follow.

"Hey wait up! I was only joking, *mon amie*," she called.

Car ran up behind me, threw her arms around me, and kissed my cheek. Just friends—*right*. We had momentarily paused midway at a crosswalk on Telegraph Avenue and a car honked at us to stop blocking traffic. I pushed Carmelita's arms away.

"Quit it, Car. Stop. People'll get ideas about us. Plus, we'll cause traffic accidents."

"Someone got up on the wrong side of the bed this morning."

We were silent for the next few blocks. Then suddenly I remembered my dream, the one I had been having before it morphed into the one with Sal and Dean at Vesuvio.

Carmelita had been in it.

I suddenly felt my face turn red again. This reaction was starting to become part of my ongoing behavior, which I was *not* a fan of.

I quickened my pace and decided that I would reflect upon it later, when I was no longer in the presence of Carmelita. Third period Physics would be a good time to do it. Mr. Robertson had promised to show us a *Bill Nye the Science Guy* episode that had something to do with this week's topic. I had seen every episode of that fantastic show years earlier.

We passed Weir's Weird Ice Cream Shop and I

got a sudden and strong hankering for a scoop of their famed Cedar Sage Chocolate flavor. I made a mental note to go straight there after school ended. I needed to get myself together. The news of the impending poetry club, a potential increase of Wren-dom in my life, and now my unavoidable shift in Carmelita-vibes, were all a lot to deal with. Oftentimes Weir's was the only place to go to sort everything out.

Car knew me well. She saw me eyeing Weir's and asked, "Wanna grab a cone later?"

I couldn't look her in the eye to respond but shrugged my shoulders and replied, in an attempt at nonchalance, "Dunno, maybe."

We were a block away from school now and had become part of the throngs that approached Henley High's front entrance from all directions. Most students walked, like us, or rode their bikes to school. As we got closer, I saw Wren chaining her bike up to the main bike rack. Her bike was a sky-blue color, with neon flower designs hand-painted all over it.

She rode it to and from school and her home in North Berkeley Hills, a swank section of town with killer bay views. Rumor had it that she and her dad lived in this hippie dream house with a record collection that rivaled that of Napoleon's Record Shop on University Avenue.

I momentarily considered approaching Wren and asking her about the poetry club, but I didn't want to seem overeager so decided against it. First period Lit would start in ten minutes anyway and I would probably hear about it then. Plus, I could see Tyler Jacoby coming over to me with a stack of records and didn't want to leave him hanging.

Tyler was my best friend at Henley High, apart from Carmelita. He was totally wild, with brown hair that grew and stuck out every which way, and a denim jacket with music buttons that he practically lived in. Tyler insisted on wearing his purple-lensed Beatles-style sunglasses twenty-four seven, even though he'd received detention more than ten times for doing it at school. Tyler was a total music fiend and super into collecting vintage records. I had known him since freshman year, when we had been partnered up in Biology Lab. Neither of us cared an ounce about anything science-y, other than star constellations, but Henley High had thus far failed to introduce Astronomy into the curriculum. Our mutual disinterest bonded us, as we'd spent lectures surveying each other's lists of top ten albums, top five musical acts from the early 1990s, and other such lists. It was this same mutual disinterest that had dragged us both to the chopping block when we received failing midterm grades in Bio on our progress reports.

Both of us being semi-nerds, Tyler and I made a pact that we would lock up our record collections and forego all list-making until the end of the semester. We would study, seriously, all of our Bio coursework until after the final exam. It soon became clear that Tyler had been speaking most literally about the lock-up. The following Saturday he showed up at my house with the hugest padlock and bike chain I'd ever seen and proceeded to pack up all of my records into a cardboard box, lock them up, and throw the key out into my mom's peony garden. It was a lot of fun trying to find that key when the summer began and Tyler and I were once again free men, free to listen to as many records as we pleased. It took us three and a half days to find it.

Tyler and I were audiophiles and Holy Vinylists; thus, we were against listening to music via any means other than vinyl records and live performances. All of those online music streaming sites and illegal downloads altered what Tyler called "the ideal sound."

About once a month, usually on a Monday morning, Tyler arrived at school with five or six albums to lend me, most of which I had never heard of. He worked part-time at Napoleon's and had set up a sort of library-loan deal with Napoleon himself so that he didn't have to blow all his dough on record purchases. When I pointed out that this was a similar method to many of our friends who down-loaded music online, in that none of us was paying for it, Tyler insisted that I was wrong.

"We're on the level. What you're talking about, amigo, is straight-up stealing. And that is never, ever, cool," he had told me.

I agreed, of course.

This particular Monday morning, Tyler shoved a stack of jazz records into my arms. He was chewing on a toothpick and wearing his purple-lensed shades, as he always was. Tyler was a true individual kid. I surveyed the records, some of whose cardboard covers were half-disintegrated.

"Thanks, Tyler."

"You got it, Ziv. Good weekend?"

I thought about the question as Carmelita watched me with a raised eyebrow. She was used to me thinking too hard about simple and common-place questions.

"Yeah, not bad. We went to North Beach

yesterday, hit up City Lights. Saw Bobcat at Vesuvio. He says hi."

Tyler grinned and chewed on his toothpick as he answered.

"Bobby! Oh man, I miss him. It's been way too long since I've been to North Beach. Got to get back there soon. These Napoleon shifts have been taking over my life. Hey Car, how goes it?"

Carmelita pocketed her aviators and smiled. "It goes, Tyler, it certainly goes."

The morning warning bell rang then, urging all remaining students, us included, to get the heck inside a classroom within the next five minutes if we didn't want to get a late-date on our permanent records. Three of those in a semester and a kid would be facing detention, which meant early-morning Saturday school cleanup sessions. Nobody wanted that.

Tyler, Carmelita, and I hurried inside and toward our locker section at the end of the first-floor hallway. It was the best spot in the school and the three of us had sought it out on the first day of classes this year. Locker assignments at Henley High worked as an every-man-for-himself sort of deal each year. A student could claim any locker as his own by throwing a lock on it.

As I gathered the necessary books for my morning classes, I saw Tyler unlock a secondary locker next to his own. In it appeared to be dozens more records. He gazed at the stacks, patted them lovingly, sighed in satisfaction, and then relocked them up.

"How long before somebody realizes you're locker-hogging?"

"How long does infinity last? Because that's how long it'll be before somebody realizes."

"You awe me."

"Thank you, man, thank you."

"Do you even have a record player here at Henley to use those records? Can't you leave them at home?"

"I like having them close by. Plus, it makes for

easy transit to and from Napoleon's when I do my afterschool shifts."

"You guys do know that the Internet exists, right?" Carmelita asked. "And that any song you could think of would be obtainable within its dimensions? I mean—do you even have *cellphones*?"

"Of course we do," I replied, because we did. I had an iPhone but I tried not to overuse it. Tyler had an old-school flip-phone and refused to utilize its internet functions. He didn't even have a Facebook account. He only had an email account because Henley High made it mandatory for school-related communications. Tyler was my role model for what we called "timeless existence." Tyler aimed to live in a way that could easily be transferred to another era, past or future. Direct experience. This was modeled after some of the Beat writers' philosophies. Tyler was not one hundred percent realistic. But he was one hundred percent into time travel.

The real first period bell rang and Tyler and I ran

to the nearby classroom where Ms. Reese held her Lit lectures. We took our seats next to Carmelita in the second row near the window. Ms. Reese's classroom was set up in such a way as to encourage mental relaxation—or so she said. All of the seats were mismatched armchairs, dining room chairs, and even a few ottomans. On the walls, in addition to the student work being showcased on rotation, there were posters of the books that we would be reading during the semester, and great black-and-white photographs of old San Francisco.

Ms. Reese had an awesome past. She used to live on the Mojave Desert and wrote two novels and a play—*by hand*, on scraps of paper—while she was there. One night, right when she was finishing the play, an intense desert wind came along and blew all of her pages out into oblivion. She said that she wept for four hours, then pulled herself together, packed up all of her junk, and split. She hitchhiked to Berkeley and never looked back. Now she was our teacher and was engaged to a sculptor who was getting to be pretty famous, or so she told us. Ms. Reese had also published three other books since her desert experience, but I felt that the desert story summed up her character pretty well. If that catastrophe had happened to me and my books, I might not have been so cool and calm.

I took my essay out of my bag, along with my Lit notebook, Nathaniel Hawthorne's *The Scarlet Letter*, and my favorite pen. Ms. Reese came into the room and began to write the daily plan on the dry erase board. I was trying to decipher her untidy scrawl when I felt a soft tap on my back. I turned around to see.

It was Wren. She looked beautiful wearing a Doors t-shirt, and her long dark curls were swept up with a large white gardenia.

"Hey, Hunter. Your hair looks extra-neat today." She smiled wide.

And it began again—my face burned in what I imagined to be a crimson hue. I cleared my throat to distract her.

"Oh, thanks, thanks a lot. I uh—washed it, I guess." This was true, I had washed it this morning. Sal the Cat was my witness.

Tyler turned to survey the scene. He kept silent but offered me a raised eyebrow—a reminder to keep it extra-cool. I changed topics.

"So, is it true you're starting a poetry club? Or Ms. Reese is? Or something like that?"

Wren raised her eyebrow and turned to go sit on her ottoman, saying to me, "Well you'll just have to wait and see, won't you?"

Tyler nudged me hard in the ribs. "Beware of the hippified hipstress, my man."

I didn't quite know how to respond; I wasn't sure what was going on myself. It seemed that A) a new and exciting writing outlet was in the process of forming at Henley High, and B) Wren may or may not have been openly flirting with me. If these two storylines intersected, I could turn out to be one lucky man.

The sound of Ms. Reese's finger cymbals jarred me back to the present moment. I was saved from having to respond to Tyler for now.

Ms. Reese always began class this way. She had super-long blonde hair and these kooky purple glasses, and she tended to wear flowing scarves and skirts.

"How was everyone's weekend?" she asked all of us. The fact that it was first period on a Monday meant that basically no one answered. There were about twenty of us in Honors Lit and there were about twelve of us who hadn't quite woken up yet.

Kate Shankar's eyes were actually closed. Julian Frey sat cross-legged on his ottoman, but his head kept nodding back and jerking forward every time he realized that he was falling asleep.

Ms. Reese smiled at the silence and went on. She was the most tolerant teacher that I had come across yet. There was a mutual sort of allowing and acceptance in her class—most of us liked Ms. Reese and the literature that we studied. Plus, we were all nerdy kids, at least about English—the Honors bunch of Junior Year. It was kind of a shame that our class met during first period, when we weren't even warmed up into the day yet. But Henley High's scheduling office wasn't exactly a flexible operation.

"Glad to hear you all had such great weekends . . . mine went way too fast, of course. How did the essays go?"

An assortment of mumbled replies arose from all of us in response.

"Glad to hear that too . . . think I'll start serving

coffee here in the morning so that we can all speak in complete sentences. Pass your papers up to me, please, and then we have some announcements."

We all passed our essays forward to the Turn-it-in Table at the front of the room and Ms. Reese went on.

"Now before we get into our discussion of Hester Prynne and Dimmesdale and the whole *Scarlet Letter* gang, I have some exciting news about a new extracurricular club here at Henley. Well, *we* do. Wren?"

Wren stood up and went to the front of the room. I sat forward in my patchwork armchair to listen. This was going to be good.

A lilting breeze came in through the opened window. Ms. Reese's nearby chimes rung softly in response. Wren began.

"So, since moving here to Berkeley, I've gotten super into poetry and especially Beat poetry and spoken word. You know, writing that sounds even better when spoken out loud? Stuff that sounds like music. And the North Beach area, right over the Golden Gate Bridge there, is chock *full* of history, the history of Beat poetry. So much happened, right there. What better way to celebrate this history than to do it again now, to bring it back?"

I stole a glance at Carmelita; her gaze was narrowed in skepticism. Myself—well, I couldn't help but be excited by Wren's speech.

"I spoke to Ms. Reese about starting a club here at Henley High—a poetry club for juniors," she went on. "We'll meet after school once a week at Caffe Trieste on Vallejo and have readings there. To be in the club, you have to write a new poem every week. The first meeting will be this Thursday and it'll be more of an intro meeting, an audition. Ms. Reese always talks about peer support during our editing process, and I think to have that same support system in the club, we'll all have to approve of all of the members' creative work. So . . . it's gonna be really fantastic. Hope to see everybody Thursday!"

Wren sat back down in her seat, beaming from ear to ear.

"Thank you, Wren," said Ms. Reese. "I think that this is a wonderful opportunity for all of you to experience the support of your fellow writers, and to appreciate the artistic legacy of where you happen to live!"

"Will you be there, Ms. Reese?" Carmelita asked.

"No—no, I teach a photography course at the Art Exchange on Thursday afternoons. I will be reading your turned-in work, surely, and I will be there with you in spirit of course. I look forward to hearing all about your progress."

Carmelita nudged me and whispered, "I don't know about this."

I shrugged in response and focused back on Wren. Three days until Thursday. Three days wasn't that much time to write the best poem in the entire world but I would do my best.

I looked around the room and caught Wren's

eye. She mouthed, "See?" and gave me a big smile. My face felt like it went up in flames.

———

During lunch period Tyler, Carmelita, and I staked our usual piece of lawn outside. We discussed the poetry club news as we grazed on home-brought items. Tyler was all psyched up about it. Carmelita wasn't.

"She's trying to do an open hippie poetry collective, right, but what kind of peace-and-love world uses auditions? And who's going to decide who gets to stay in? *Her*, right?"

Carmelita took an angry bite of her pita bread. I was getting angry myself. Car didn't even know Wren. Who was she to suggest that Wren was an ego-based judgmental creep? She finished the pita and began crunching away at her apple. I noticed Tyler frowning slightly as he watched Carmelita in action; he didn't say anything though. Car went on.

"And I'm sure *she's* already in, right? No audition for her because it was her stupid idea. I mean—she *just* moved here! What does she know about North Beach, the Beat poets, Jack Kerouac and Allen Ginsberg and Neal Cassady? *We* grew up here! *We* were born right here in Berkeley!"

Now I felt my face turning red again but not because I was embarrassed.

Tyler spoke. "If I didn't know any better, I'd say you were jealous of Wren's idea. That you're jealous of *her*, even."

This is what I had suspected too and wanted to say but couldn't. I hadn't wanted to get into a dialogue about it. I had just wanted Carmelita to stop. I'd known her for what seemed like forever and I'd seen her like this before. Not often, because she was, as a rule, pretty cool, as I tried to be. My guess was that she had issues with Wren of a grand order, issues that I didn't want to involve myself in unless I had to.

Tyler waited for Carmelita to respond but she

seemed to be giving us the silent treatment. I forked up the rest of Mom's tofu rice leftovers and went to throw out my trash in the can at the bottom of the hill. I needed to breathe for a moment, on my own, away from the Carmelita rant that was in progress. From my stance on the hill I could see Wren and a couple of her friends, mostly guys in the afterschool music program, having lunch on the other side of the field.

I wanted something new. I wanted to take the next step, to make a leap, to become the artist, the writer that I really wanted to be, that I was meant to be. I felt so sure that this new poetry club was a step in the right direction. I felt so sure that Wren was.

I returned to my place with Carmelita and Tyler. Both were silent now. I suddenly felt sad and frustrated. Didn't Carmelita understand what a big deal this was—working on creative material, being part of a writers' collective, doing readings at Caffe Trieste? It would make Jack Kerouac's ghost proud!

"Tyler," I said, "what do you think?"

He was lying on his back, tearing a blade of grass in two.

"About what?" he responded, looking at me upside-down, squinting in the sharp sunlight.

"The new poetry club that . . . that Ms. Reese mentioned. Are you gonna do it? Are you gonna go on Thursday to the meeting?"

"If I can get out of my shift at Napoleon's, man. He's been running me ragged as of late. That's because Anita—"

"—oh yeah, the crazy chick—"

"—she's on vacation this week. I'm taking over all of her shifts, plus my own. This weekend I am working two doubles—Saturday *and* Sunday. May Earth and Sky help me."

Tyler was a self-dubbed naturalist. He considered his religion to be of the earth, so instead of using God's name in vain, he would go the other route.

Carmelita had opened her Physics textbook and was now reading with her nose buried in the pages. I was surprised that she could even see the words that close up. I asked her anyway.

"Car. Are you gonna go?"

She waited a few seconds too long to respond. "Go where?"

"To the poetry club meeting at Caffe Trieste. On Thursday."

Carmelita put the book down and looked at me over her shades. I felt a chill go through my body.

"Yeah, I guess I have to. Can't let you two bozos go unsupervised, all the way to the city and back."

The bell rang loudly and we hurried to grab our books and junk from off the lawn. Carmelita had Physics next; Tyler and I had Trigonometry. We walked to the main building in silence as the afternoon sun burned high above us. Although the weather in the main city across the bay was all over the place and varied from neighborhood to neighborhood, Berkeley weather was more or less decidedly sunny and bright for most of the time.

We approached the main inner stairwell and

paused; Tyler and I had to go up to the second floor and Carmelita's class was in the basement.

"See you later, Car? After school to walk home?" I asked.

She looked at me with a deadpan expression on her face. "No, that's okay, thanks. I'd prefer to do my own thing today."

I felt my face grow red and hot but hoped that it would quickly subside. I wasn't sure what was going on with Carmelita and me. Nothing, I guessed.

She was gone down the stairs just like that. I looked at Tyler.

"You know where I have to be after school, Ziv. Napoleon's. Tonight I've got to totally reorganize the Blues section of the store. Do you *know* how long that's going to take me?"

We climbed the stairs to the second floor and walked down the hall toward the Trig room.

"Uber-long, Ziv. I might be there past midnight."

We plunked ourselves down in last-row desks

as Mr. Kim, our teacher, began writing the daily prompt on the board. I momentarily regretted spending so much time on Ms. Reese's essay last night, when I should have been studying Trig. I had done the homework hastily during breakfast yesterday morning while Mom and Dad tried to book plane tickets to conferences that they had to attend next month in Philadelphia and Baltimore, respectively.

I took a deep breath, reminding myself that my career as a literary artist trumped any other sort of assignment that could ever arise for me. I chose to calm down. I would get by in Trig; I studied enough and had received As and a few Bs thus far.

As Mr. Kim finished writing out the prompt I considered potential subjects for my audition poem, the one that I would write later, after school.

—

It was six fifteen that night when I threw another

balled-up piece of paper over my shoulder. It was the fourth piece of trash—and the fourth aborted writing attempt of mine thus far—and I had been working for over an hour in the common area of our apartment building. The area was on the roof and offered pretty cool views of San Francisco Bay, the main city, and Berkeley. I sipped the cup of chamomile tea that I had brought up with me. The label on the box in my kitchen assured the user that it would "relax and soothe," both of which I would accept for my audition poem-writing process.

I wanted to keep the tone of my poem as true to myself as possible. I wanted it to be tough and gruff and wise and humorous. I knew that it wouldn't rhyme; I didn't want it to.

Settling on a subject to write about was difficult. I went back and forth between stuff about the beauty and harmony of Muir Woods, and my escapade with Mara in freshman year. And Wren. I wanted to write about her most of all, but I also knew that she would be reading it and hesitated to try to articulate how I truly felt about her.

I finished the tea and stood up from the wooden bench to stretch my legs. The lights on the Golden Gate glimmered. I felt inspired, as I always did from living here. But inspired to do what, exactly? What would I write?

Just then I heard the roof door open and turned to see who had come in. Ramon and Amelia appeared with books in hand.

"Hey, Hunter," Ramon said. "How's it going?"

"Okay, I guess. Trying to write. How about you guys?"

"Trying to study," Amelia answered. They sat across from me and opened up their textbooks.

"What are you writing?" Ramon asked.

"A poem—but not the usual poem. Not flowery or anything. Like a Beat poem, a prose-ish sort of thing."

Amelia smiled. "Nice. For a girl?"

I looked away into the distance. "I don't know,

maybe. It's for a club at school. There're auditions for it on Thursday and I have to bring in a poem of mine."

"Well, I'm not big into poetry or anything," Ramon said as he put his arm around Amelia, "but when I have to write, I try to think of a phrase or line that I like first and go from there, instead of thinking about the content too much. I like to go with what I'm feeling, you know?"

Suddenly I knew what I would write. I needed to get to a place of solitude, and fast. I grabbed my scattered pages and tea and went for the stairs.

"Hey, where are you—" Ramon started to ask.

"Thanks so much for all the help, Ramon. I've got to go."

"Good night," Amelia called as I hurried down the steps.

I didn't stop to respond.

On the first day of the poetry club, Caffe Trieste's interior was dimly lit, even for an afternoon when the sun was still up. Tawny and cherry-colored wooden walls were covered with rows of black-and-white photos much like Ms. Reese's. The smell of espresso beans radiated throughout the room.

Fewer students had turned up for this first meeting than I had imagined would. About seven or eight of us were scattered throughout the place, listening to Wren speak in the center of the room. Will was by her side, nodding at everything that she said. Will was one of the music students with whom Wren always hung out.

I couldn't imagine that he was much of a writer. I remembered him from sophomore year when he had tried to organize a student protest against price increases on Henley High's vending machines. For two weeks he'd spent every morning outside the front entrance screaming from atop a milk crate and handing out flyers on student rights to passersby. Will was a bit over the top for my taste.

Some 1950s jazz played softly over the stereo system. There seemed to be a couple of non-Henley High folks at the countertop area—vaguely disgruntled-looking old men sipping cappuccinos and reading newspapers intensely. I thought of the Beats hanging out here years ago, all of their innovative ideas coming together, soon to change the philosophy of literature, of the world. I wanted to do that myself, with Wren, here, now. The possibilities seemed endless.

Carmelita and Tyler took seats with Kate Shankar and her boyfriend. Car had been silent during the entire BART ride while Tyler riffed on Beatles records. Apparently he had gotten into an argument with Napoleon about which album of theirs was the best one. Knowing Tyler as I did, I wouldn't have been surprised if the whole thing went on and on as a philosophical conundrum for weeks.

Wren stood up, took a deep breath with eyes closed, and rang a pair of finger cymbals three times in sequence. She must have borrowed them from Ms. Reese.

All were silent and directed their attention to Wren. Several of the students who had shown up clutched their entry poems nervously, crinkling the pages and clearing their throats. I chose the path of calmness instead. I knew that the poem I held in my hands would garner my entry into this club.

She opened her eyes and spoke. "Welcome every-one and thank you for coming. This is the first meeting of the Henley High Poetry Club. Most of you heard about it in Ms. Reese's class. We'll be jamming together, literarily speaking, here at Caffe Trieste every Thursday after school. At the end of the semester we'll have a showcase performance with everyone's best work read out loud. The purpose of this club is to become better at writing and to enjoy each other's work. To have fun, too."

She looked at Will and they both laughed; I scowled. Will wouldn't know a good piece of writing if it bit him in the—

"Ms. Reese, an actual published author, will serve as our presiding faculty member. But she is being super-cool about it, letting us all run the meetings ourselves. Remember, this is supposed to be a totally free, creative, artistic expression zone. It's not school, there are no grades, and there's no judgment here! We just want to create."

Carmelita snorted in disbelief. I looked to see if Wren had noticed—it seemed that she hadn't, but Will was eyeing our section of the room suspiciously. Wren went on.

"So let's get started. Did everyone bring a first poem to submit?"

There was a rustling of papers as people dug through their bags and passed their poems forward. I smoothed mine out and gave it a last onceover. I had used my Underwood typewriter and this fancy weathered-looking paper that I kept around for special occasions. It was ready for Wren's eyes, I knew.

Suddenly someone grabbed the paper out of my hand. I looked up to see Will. He smiled a forced smile.

"We don't have all day, Zivsky."

My fists clenched slowly but stayed where they were on my lap. This kid had some nerve and was lucky to be dealing with a mellow cat like myself.

"It's *Zivotovsky*," I corrected him, but he had already returned to Wren, who was shaking the pages into a uniformed pile.

"Thank you, thank you, verrrrrry cool. Will, ready?"

He nodded as Wren divided the stack in half and then gave one portion to Will. There was an elongated pause and for a moment I wondered what was going on—until Wren and Will tore their respective stacks into two, then four, then eight and then a million little pieces of paper. All of us in the audience seemed to gasp in horror at the same time.

"Don't!" yelled Kate Shankar.

"Oh my *God*—ridiculous," exclaimed Carmelita.

My heart sank with the awareness that the only copy of the world's best poem written by me had just been destroyed in front of my own eyes. I had typed it on the Underwood to achieve a greater authenticity, imagining that I would get the paper back at some point. Now it was lost to history. No wonder Carmelita always wrote on her laptop.

Three kids who were part of the music scene at Henley stood up and grabbed their jackets. Two of them shrugged at each other and left; the other stayed behind when Will shot him a disapproving look.

He and Wren gathered up the bits of paper and put them into a garbage bag. Wren smiled.

"You might be wondering why we did that."

"You bet we are. That was the only poem I brought with me," Kate snarked.

"Well, here's why," Wren answered. "See that photo over there?"

She pointed to a curling poster on the far wall of the cafe. It was a popular one, available for purchase at City Lights Bookstore, with an image of young Jack Kerouac and Neal Cassady together. I had always loved that image.

"Jack and Neal and the Beat Poets worked by the philosophy of 'first thought, best thought.'"

This was true; I wondered, though, if any of them had ever been forced to watch their own work torn up in front of them.

"So that'll be our main creative creed here,"

Wren continued, "and we're only going to write instant poetry. We're doing away with drafts."

This I liked; drafts and I did not get along. Would Ms. Reese be a supporter of this, though? It seemed to me that we spent a lot of her classes in peer review sessions, which led to the construction of two drafts and sometimes even three.

"Every week, every meeting," Will added, "we'll each write a new poem in twenty minutes without editing, and then we'll share them with each other. Let's do that now, in fact."

Will passed out paper and pens. Carmelita took them but didn't start writing; instead, she looked around at all of us and at Wren in disbelief.

"Why did we have to bring in a new poem just for it to be destroyed? Was that *really* necessary?"

Wren looked uncomfortable but didn't answer. Car spoke to the group again.

"You're all gonna go in for this, everybody? *Crazy* antics done in the name of creativity?"

"Come on, Car," Tyler interjected. "We're here.

We ought to give it a shot. It'll be an interesting experiment in any case."

Carmelita seized a pen and paper and started to write. I grabbed my pen. After several moans of annoyance, the room grew quiet as people started to write. What were they writing about? It didn't matter; I had to focus here and now. What ideas did I have filed away, ideas that I could use now? I threw my fishing line into the cool mountain stream that was my creative zone, but nothing seemed to be swimming there at the moment. I truly felt that I had put *all* of my creative energy into writing the poem that I wrote last night. I never imagined in a million years that I would get there and have to write another one! This was starting to feel like taking an exam—an exam that I hadn't studied for. I began to panic.

Suddenly I inhaled a fresh scent of lilac and looked up to see Wren smiling at me. She seemed to give off a glow of calm and positivity at all times. I tried to soak up some of it myself, thinking that it would help me in my writing. She carried a stack of paper cups and a pitcher with some kind of purplish iced drink inside.

"Chamomile-lavender iced tea? I made it myself. I always drink it when I'm writing. It helps for relaxation and lets the best ideas rise to the surface."

I hoped to Jack Kerouac's ghost that she was right and poured myself a large glass. Perhaps this entire setup, perhaps the surprise poetry pop quiz, had been established by Wren as a sort of romantic test of chivalry, an opportunity for me to prove my worthiness to her. Yes, *yes*, I thought as I looked at Tyler furrowing his brow over pages, and Carmelita writing furiously, hunched over the table. Yes, this was the only explanation.

Well, I wouldn't disappoint her. I took another glance at Wren across the room. The fibers on her gold scarf caught the rays of afternoon sun that streamed through the window. She laughed melodically as Tyler whispered something in her ear—what, I couldn't tell. She pushed his arm playfully and I felt my anger rising. No, I wouldn't disappoint her at all.

Just like that, the words came. One after another after another. Each sentence seemed to have a rhythm and the timing was perfect—the *second* that the feeling came to me, my mind was right there to articulate it and my hand was there to pen it. This went on and on for what seemed like forever, but I kept writing. My hand ached from gripping the ballpoint, whose ink was running dry. I didn't second-guess any word or line that I chose—there wasn't time. This, I realized, *this* was how Jack must have felt when he threw forth *On the Road* to that winding scroll of paper—at one with the forces of the universe. This feeling was why I had chosen to be a writer.

The finger-cymbals clanged once again and Will spoke.

"All right guys, it's time to put the pens down and pass your papers forward. Give thanks for the awesome words that you've written and send them up here!"

We all turned our pages in as Wren and Will began to leaf through them, stopping here and there to look more closely at a rhyme or phrase. I looked around the cafe; the other patrons seemed to have left. One forlorn-looking barista wiping the counter-top remained. The same low-key jazz music played; funny that I hadn't heard it while I was writing. Probably a good sign; I must have been focusing to the utmost degree.

"That was intense, man," Tyler said to me. "Not sure that I like the whole 'surprise' angle. I do *not* like to be rushed, you know? But we shall see."

He yawned and stretched his legs out in front of him. Carmelita played tic-tac-toe with Kate on some of the extra paper but she didn't look too enthusiastic. Then Will spoke and our attention was drawn back to the poem-sorting.

"Hey everyone, this work all looks really

fantastic. There's one in particular . . . We should read it out loud, I guess."

Wren had pulled one piece of paper from the pile.

"There's one poem here that we think is just so super-great, and most definitely in the spirit of the Beats and Jack," she said. "I'm going to read it out loud as a stellar example of what we want in this club—if that's okay with the author. Hunter, do you mind?"

I was speechless; I hadn't expected this, either. I felt my face get a bit flushed again—and at my moment of glory, too.

"Nah, I don't mind," I replied, keeping my cool. I was aware that most of the heads in the room were turned toward me but I tried not to care and just focused on Wren. She began to read:

"*new to me*
new in town
flavors of fevers from the word go
flowers in her hair were enough to catch me

match me make me want

to get up to that house on the hill…"

Hearing Wren speak the words that I had just written made me feel like I was dreaming. Every once in a while as she moved through the stanzas she would look up and out into the audience. Every once in a while she would catch my eye. Her eyebrows raised as her voice paused and then restarted, grew louder and quieter, quickened its speed and then slowed down. She read it with a jazzed-up sense of rhythm that the Beats would have been proud of.

When she finished, everyone clapped, even Will—though reluctantly so.

"Well, our hour is up and we have to get the heck out of the Caffe now," Wren said. "But we hope to see you all back here next week, when we'll have some discussion about our first poems from today, and write more new ones. Also if anyone hasn't read *Howl* by Allen Ginsberg, we suggest reading it before next week. It's not too long and is more or less essential to have read in order to be a San Franciscan poet."

"She isn't a San Franciscan poet; she's not *from* here," Carmelita said under her breath. People began to gather their jackets and books and head for the door.

"Uh . . . hold on a second . . . Carmelita?"

Will stopped her as she headed for the door. "Can I talk to you a second?" he asked and motioned to a corner of the cafe. Carmelita went along but seemed to be suspicious. I was about to head over there too but was stopped by Wren.

"Hey there. I love love *loved* your poem, Hunter. You're an incredible writer. I'm glad you're doing this with us."

I looked off to the side for dramatic effect.

"Well thanks, thanks a lot. I am too. Whatever you put in that tea, it works."

Wren laughed and fiddled with the sleeve of my Army jacket. She spoke in a singsong voice and kind of looked at the floor as she went on.

"Well, anytime you want more, I'd be happy to supply it. I'm making it for my Dad's book party on Saturday night, in fact."

I'd always wanted to go to a book party. From what I could tell, it was an event when the author invited all of his pals to an over-the-top celebration for the release of his new book.

"I didn't know that your dad had a new book coming out."

"Yeah, he's been working on this one for a while. Maybe . . . well, you might have plans . . . "

"I don't have plans," I replied back, way too quickly. This coolness thing was hard to manage.

"Well, great. Do you think you can come? It starts at seven."

I paused for a moment so as not to seem too eager.

"Um . . . yeah, I think I can make it."

Wren smiled. Was it just my imagination, or did she seem a bit nervous too?

"Lovely."

She hesitated for a moment and then pulled a Carmelita. Wren kissed me on the cheek. And suddenly Carmelita was at my side, speaking.

"Are you ready to go yet? Tyler and I can't really wait around all night."

Car didn't seem mad, but there was something in her eyes that I hadn't really seen before.

I cleared my throat and followed her to the door.

"Bye!" Wren mouthed to me through the window as we left.

I was over the moon. But as we walked toward the BART stop to head back to Berkeley, I could tell that something was wrong with Car.

"So, that was pretty cool, right? What did you guys think?"

Both of them were silent for a moment.

Tyler spoke first. "I'll say one thing's for sure: those two really go in for theatrics."

"Well," I explained, "the Beat poets were into speaking their work out loud. The performance of the work mattered. They probably went in for theatrics too."

Tyler shook his head. "I don't know, man—tearing up our work right in front of us? It would be one thing if they were Mr. Kim's dumb Trig worksheets, but they were poems. More . . . sensitive, you know? That part seemed, well, *nutso.*"

Carmelita looked a bit faraway in the eyes.

"I think that they were just trying to get us amped up, excited, you know? What did you think, Car?"

At my question she focused and asked, "It was about her, wasn't it?"

Tyler jumped in. "Oh yeah, Hunter, your poem was awesome. Really great. Can't wait to hear your next one."

"Hunter?" Carmelita prompted.

I wished she'd leave it alone; I didn't want to talk about it. It felt private. I didn't like hiding things from Carmelita, but I wanted to keep Wren and how I felt about her to myself. I hastily formed a response.

"Ah well, you know, writers are inspired by all different stuff, all of the time. Especially poetry. It doesn't always make sense, Car. I just went with . . . what *came* to me."

We had reached the station and were now waiting on the platform. The next train was due in one minute. Carmelita lightly touched my arm.

"But, 'flowers in her hair'? 'New in town,' 'house on the hill'? That's all Wren."

I looked down at my sneakers, not sure what to say. Had it been that obvious? If I'd had a chance to review it, I might have tried to be more ambiguous about the idea of the poem. But Wren had been standing right in front of me—what else should I have been inspired by?

"Come on, Carmelita. That's not 'all Wren,' it's just whatever, all right? It's from me, from my own mind, my own pen and paper. Give me more credit than that. I never write so literally."

Car still eyed me curiously with the same sadness; Tyler said nothing.

The train came whooshing into the station. We boarded and found three seats together. Carmelita closed her eyes and rested her head on Tyler's shoulder.

She usually did that with me.

6

Banking on Carmelita's usual lateness, the next morning I took my time getting to the lawn of our complex. It was Friday and I was feeling fine and proud of myself for how well I had done yesterday at the poetry club meeting, and looking forward to Saturday and Wren's dad's book party. The sun shone brightly and I could smell the dew on the blades beneath my sneakers. I took a deep breath in and savored the moment, beginning to get an idea for my next poem.

As I approached the bottom of the hill I was met with a plot twist: Carmelita was already there in her aviators, reading what appeared to be a copy of Donna Tartt's *The Goldfinch*.

"Just some light reading for a Friday morning, huh? Starting the weekend right?" I joked.

She looked up and smiled but her tone was serious.

"That idiot from yesterday recommended it. I figured that he couldn't be all wrong. This thing did win the Pulitzer after all. Apparently it should be up my literary alley."

She stood up and we took off on our usual route.

"Which idiot—Will? Oh yeah, is this what he needed to speak to you about yesterday?"

My encounter with Wren following the meeting had caused me to totally forget about Carmelita and Will. I suddenly became very curious. What if he had invited Car out somewhere? Anything seemed to be possible as of late, so it wasn't totally out of the question.

"Apparently," Car explained, "my stuff is too

dark, heavy, and Dickensian for this club's creed of lightness and positivity."

"He said that to you?"

"In not so many words, yes."

That total *idiot*. I knew that he wasn't to be trusted.

"He can't do that to you! Tell Ms. Reese! Tell—"

"—Wren? I doubt that she would be of much help. Honestly, I don't really care. I think it's a dumb idea anyway. I'm not going to stop writing. That kid, Will, suggested that what I wrote wasn't true. But what I wrote was true. It was true for me; it was how I felt at the time. I was pissed off! I worked really hard on the poem that they tore up. I know that everyone had, but I couldn't move on so easily."

We passed Weir's and I remembered my promise to buy myself a cedar sage chocolate cone. I would do it over the weekend. Maybe I would bring a pint to the book party.

"I get it," I responded. "Sorry that Will was so obnoxious."

"It's fine. I just wish—I just wish that you felt the same about it."

"I do feel the same! Will is a total jerk!"

"No, I mean the whole shebang, the club and its plans. I wish we agreed about it, that's all. I'm kind of surprised. I thought I knew you. It makes me nervous that we don't agree."

Just then a swift and direct October breeze picked up, seeming to come in from off the mountains somewhere near Grizzly Peak. The trees on University Avenue swayed, their branches bending and yielding.

So this was how change felt. It didn't feel comfortable at all and I wasn't sure that I was okay with it.

We were quiet for a while. Carmelita checked her phone as we stopped at a red light. She laughed at what seemed to be an incoming text and smiled as she typed a response. I wondered who it was from, but Car wasn't volunteering that information. I almost asked her, but suddenly every potential phrasing sounded awkward or forced in my mind.

We approached the block of Henley and saw Tyler sauntering around near the entrance. He was talking to Julian Frey. Even though Julian was in Ms. Reese's class too and liked writing, especially screenplay stuff, he hadn't been at the club meeting yesterday. I had always liked Julian. He was kind of a quiet kid, but when he did say something it was always pretty smart. His observational powers were intense.

"Hey, Tyler. Hey, Julian. Where were you yesterday?" I asked.

"He's not into it," Tyler said.

"Really? But you're into writing, and you love Jack Kerouac. Isn't *The Dharma Bums* your favorite book?"

A warning bell rang from inside and we all began to walk toward the entrance.

"This is true," Julian said. "But the moment I heard that kid Will was involved I lost interest."

"See?" said Carmelita.

"Yes, he's annoying," I added, "but the club still seems like it might be a good place to try out material and stuff."

"Nah, I don't think so. It doesn't give me good vibes."

This was troubling to me. Had he forgotten about Wren? She was *made* of good vibes.

"What about Wren?" I asked. Carmelita looked at me but quickly turned away. She hurried ahead toward the lockers.

"Yeah, her too," said Julian. "I like how 'out there' she is, and she is easy on the eyes. But there's something unreal about her—and not in a good way."

We approached the classroom and found our seats. I looked around for Wren but she didn't seem to be there yet.

"Any weekend plans?" Tyler asked me.

"Going to a book party, I think."

"A book party? Far out, where at?"

"It's for Wren's dad. I think it's at her house."

Tyler smiled and raised an eyebrow at me.

"Ah yes, your girl's house."

"Hey, she's not really my girl—"

"Well whatever she is, just tread cautiously, my man."

"What do you mean?"

"Just . . . don't rush in. Keep your cool for a while. I got a bad feeling yesterday with her and Will. And what they did to Carmelita, man? Not fair."

I was starting to get a bit ticked off. Suddenly no one liked this new adventure. Why were they being stubborn? Nobody trusted Wren, for *absolutely* no reason at all. Didn't they see what I saw?

"And Julian doesn't dig it either. He's usually on the ball with that stuff."

"Yeah well, *he wasn't there*. And they really liked my poem."

"It was great, Hunter. You know I love your stuff. Just don't let your ego, you know, *skew* everything—"

"Hey, my ego's fine."

Tyler put his hands up in surrender. "I'm sure it is man, I'm sure it is."

The last bell rang and Ms. Reese came waltzing into the room. Wren was with her and wore a green dress made of different patches of fabric that looked like a cascade of Redwood tree leaves. My face felt hot and I tried to keep cool in my spot on the otto-man. My shoulders were practically up to my ears in tension from the conversations with Carmelita, Julian, and Tyler. I sure could use some of Wren's relaxation iced tea.

"Good morning, everyone," said Ms. Reese as she started to write some upcoming due dates for assign-ments on the board. "How did the club meeting go yesterday?"

"It was super awesome, Ms. Reese. Some extra

creative vibes were flowing for sure. Hunter wrote an incredible poem," said Wren.

"Well done, Hunter! I'd love to read it. That reminds me—I have some exciting news. In conjunction with this new extracurricular, the Lit department here at Henley High has decided to hold a junior year poetry contest!"

The excitement in the room was palpable. Wren beamed from ear to ear; Carmelita nudged me and said, "You'd better enter this thing."

"Entries—one poem per person—are due by next Friday and you can drop them off at the Literature office," Ms. Reese explained. "The judges will be three editors at Dandicat Press, and the winner will have his or her poem published in the Press's journal. Quite a thrilling reward. I encourage all of you here to submit something into the contest."

A poetry contest here at Henley High—publication in a real literary journal! I couldn't wait to submit something. I would have to write for the next week. Screw "first thought, best thought" for a while. I wanted my entry to be extra perfect. It would have the energy of "first thought, best thought" writing of course, but it would also have the time and attention of careful editing and revising. I wanted to cover all of my bases just to be safe.

———

On Saturday night at around six thirty, Dad and I got into the car to go to Wren's house. Dad had agreed to drive me because Wren's house was all the way up in the hills and, like many locations in the Bay Area, it was a bit difficult to reach directly via public transport.

Having never been to a book party, I hadn't been exactly sure how to dress for one. In the end I chose my best jeans and desert boots, my Grateful Dead t-shirt, and a corduroy blazer. I slicked my hair back a bit too with some fancy hair gel that I found in Mom and Dad's bathroom. It kind of smelled like high-quality paint that had sat out in the sun, but it did make me look a bit older.

Mom had suggested that I bring something to the party, so that morning I had ridden my bike to Weir's Weird Ice Cream Shop and bought a quart of their Cedar Sage Chocolate. I hoped that Wren and her dad would like it.

"Looking sharp, Hunt," my dad said as we walked to our car, which was parked across the street from the complex.

"Thanks, Dad."

As we approached the car, Ramon and Amelia came walking toward our home with stacks of books in their hands.

"Hi, Professor," Ramon said. "Hey, Hunter. We just raided the library."

"Good idea, Ramon. Excited to read your next paper. Hi, Amelia."

"Where are you guys off to?" Amelia smiled at me and I felt myself tense up in anxiousness—and just when I was trying to keep it cool in preparation for my big night, too.

"A book party, for my friend's dad."

"Sam, in the Music department," my dad added. "He's got a new book out on the history of the San Francisco music scene."

"Oh wow, that's great!" Amelia exclaimed, her eyes lighting up. "I've heard about Sam; he's got quite a reputation at Berkeley now. Didn't he date Carly Simon?"

"So the story goes," Dad answered. "Wish I could've dated her myself; I had quite a crush on her back then—"

"All right Dad, I don't want to be late," I interjected. I didn't need to hear his ramblings about Carly again—not at the moment. He was bordering on embarrassing me here in front of Amelia.

Dad snapped back to planet Earth and unlocked the car doors.

"I hear you, Hunter. Have a great night guys," he said as he put the key into the ignition.

"You too, Professor. Have a great time at the party, Hunter!" Amelia called out as she and Ramon headed into the building.

The evening was beautiful, with a cool breeze rushing through the open car windows. Streaks of orange, pink, green, and blue colored the sky above, and a star or two were just barely visible against the horizon. I couldn't wait to see Wren.

Her house was in North Berkeley Hills, a bit of a ways up from our place near the university. I usually didn't come to this part of town too much; the last time I had been was to visit my dentist. I remembered having a filling done and trying to distract myself with the panoramic views of Berkeley and the bay that the office windows offered.

As we drove down the winding roads, Dad wanted to hear all about the poetry club meeting. I told him how it had gone down—that my poem had been singled out, and that Will seemed to be a questionable character. I even told him about the public destruction of the work that we had brought in, and about the upcoming contest. And that Carmelita, Tyler, and even Julian Frey, had seemed . . . *less than excited* . . . about the whole thing.

"What would you do, Dad?"

"Well, about which part?"

I sighed in frustration. "I don't know—about how my best friends aren't into something that I'm super into, especially when it's something that they were always into before. Why don't they like Wren?"

"Well, Hunter," Dad began, before sighing and furrowing his brow. He had interrupted himself to clarify his point; I'd heard his students complain about it before. Sometimes Dad took a while to express an idea.

"People, even friends, change . . . you know," he went on.

Cars passed by us on either side of the highway. I didn't think that I was changing as fast as the cars were riding, was I? I didn't feel that different!

"I'm all for creative freedom and thinking outside of the box," Dad elaborated. His brow was furrowed in concentration. "But these kids shouldn't have gotten on Carmelita's case so fast, regardless of what they thought."

Sometimes Dad's speeches, like this one, went on forever. I hoped that he'd wrap it up soon.

"Some kids, you know, like to play teacher just a little too much. The power goes to their heads. I've had students like that."

Were Wren and Will *playing teacher*? Carmelita probably would've said so.

"You're serious about your writing too, which is, well, your mom and I are proud of you."

I didn't want this to turn into a fifties sitcom father-son act, though I did appreciate Dad's understanding.

"Thanks, Dad."

"When I was sixteen, all I did was go to concerts and get . . . well, go to concerts and chill out, let's say."

I smiled. I knew what that was code for. Dad always knew how to put things into perspective for me. It was probably the teacher in him.

We had reached the end of a long path on Buena Vista Way, the street where Wren's house was supposed to be. My dad made a right turn and suddenly we were in front of this huge and wacky-looking structure. There were high arches and all different-sized windows, seemingly placed at random—sort of like a cross between a fun house and a church. A bunch of cars were parked in the driveway and on the street, a sign that I wasn't the first guest to arrive. Music that sounded mystical and full of guitars could be heard coming from the house.

Dad and I got out of the car. I checked my bag with the ice cream for leaks. It was slightly melty but still in good shape.

"Quite a place," Dad said.

"Yep," I replied, stopping halfway up the entry

path. I didn't really want Wren to see him dropping me off.

"Well, thanks a lot for the ride, Dad. I'll see you later."

"Not so fast kiddo—I want to say hi to Sam."

I couldn't wait until Mom and Dad would let me take the car out at night on my own; according to them, I had to wait until I turned seventeen in February. I hoped that Mr. Cooper would answer the door as I rang the doorbell. After a few moments no one answered, so I knocked loudly three times.

The door swung open to reveal Wren wearing a lavender dress and a necklace made of daisies. Flower designs in glittery gold paint were drawn on her cheeks. She looked beautiful; she looked like the girl I'd always imagined myself with but never really thought existed in reality. She reached her arms out to hug me hello.

"Thanks so much for coming, Hunter. Hey, Dr. Zivotovsky! Do you want to come in? My dad is somewhere inside if you want to say hi, although everyone's all over him right now. His book is supposed to be a hit!"

"Well, that's great news. Yes, I would like to say hello, just for a moment," Dad answered.

We entered into a huge room with the highest ceilings that I'd ever seen. There were candles everywhere and white Christmas lights hanging from the rafters. People, who seemed to be a mix of familiar-looking professors I'd seen Mom and Dad with and older rock and roll stars, occupied every corner of the huge space. The music that we had heard from outside now proved to have come from a guitarist who sat playing live in the middle of the room. One long banquet table held a feast of fancy-looking appetizers and snacks, another held bottles and bottles of champagne, and one more held stacks and stacks of what must have been Mr. Cooper's new book. *Boy*, I thought, *I want my book party to be exactly like this.*

"Wow, Wren, this is amazing."

"Thank you, Hunter. Yeah, this is probably the

biggest soiree that we've had since we moved here. Hey, there's my dad! Let's go say hi."

Wren took my hand and led Dad and me over to the table of books. On the way I spotted a room to the left that appeared to house walls and walls of vinyl records. It must have been the collection that Tyler had mentioned; I wished that he could've seen it in person.

My heart thumped loudly in my chest and I hoped that the guitar music would drown it out. Mr. Cooper stood talking to a couple who appeared to be fawning over him. He was smiling, flashing actor-white teeth and listening to what the man was telling him. Wren still held my hand as we reached him.

"Hey, sweetheart," he said to her. "I'll see you later—stick around for the reading if you can, it'll happen later tonight," he told the couple as they shook his hand and walked off.

Mr. Cooper was dressed all in denim and wore motorcycle boots. His hair was shockingly white and the frames of his large eyeglasses were American flag patterned. When he saw my Dad, his face lit up and he shook his hand enthusiastically.

"Bert! How are you? I'm so glad you came."

"Good, good, it's great to see you too, Sam. Congrats on the new book. From what I hear around campus, it's supposed to hit the bestseller list in no time. And this is my son Hunter—I was dropping him off to see Wren here—"

"Hunter!" Mr. Cooper suddenly turned his attention toward me and shook my hand. "Wren's told me what a wonderful writer you are!"

I felt myself blush again. I was kind of getting used to this reaction of mine. Maybe I could work it into my act, like part of my character appeal.

"Well, I try. I'm sure you're wonderful too. I mean, you have a book party. And a book!"

I laughed nervously, but I wasn't sure my charm was working on him. Something about Mr. Cooper reminded me of a Great White Shark . . . with many teeth.

"I have several books, Hunter. This one, though, is my best yet, in my opinion. Time will tell what its effect on society and culture will be—once the reviews come in from the *Chronicle* and *The LA Times* and some East Coast outlets—"

All of a sudden Mr. Cooper seemed to notice something near my feet and pointed. His tone changed and it made me a little nervous.

"Something seems to be, uh, dripping, from your bag there. Just go into the kitchen if you could—these rugs are brand new."

How could I have forgotten—the cedar sage ice cream! I still held the quart in its shopping bag, which was now half filled with chocolate goop.

"I'm so sorry, Mr. Cooper! I meant to . . . I brought this for you. It's from Weir's Weird Ice Cream Shop. My favorite flavor."

Mr. Cooper wore a vague look of disgust on his face but seemed to catch himself and forced a smile.

"Thank you so much, Hunter, very thoughtful . . . Wren, can you take him into the kitchen, please? It's just the rugs, they're new . . ."

"Sure, Daddy. Come on, Hunter, I can show you the terrace then, too."

Wren guided me away from the ice creamed rug and into the kitchen. I felt really badly about the mess and worried that it had lessened my coolness effect. Still, Mr. Cooper seemed to be more uptight than I had imagined he would be.

On the kitchen counters were trays and trays of mini cupcakes with rainbow icing, which would go well with the ice cream, I imagined—if it hadn't completely melted. I reached into the bag and pulled the container out. It was still dripping profusely so I held it over the kitchen sink as Wren grabbed some paper towels. She started to wipe off the bottom but suddenly the whole thing slipped from my hand and dropped into the sink, splattering on the counter—and of course, onto my face.

We both froze, until Wren burst out laughing. I couldn't help but join; the moment was too hysterical.

It always seemed that when a guy tried to be his coolest self, an outside force swept in and tripped him up.

In one fast move, Wren picked up the container

again, wiped it off, and stuck it in the freezer, heaving a sigh of relief as she shut its door.

"Thank you . . . I think," she joked.

"It's really good; you'll like it. Weir's is the best."

"I kept meaning to check it out; I'm always riding my bike past the shop."

Wren gave me the onceover and raised an eyebrow before she spoke again.

"Wow, Hunter. You're a *mess*."

I looked down and saw that my shirt was splattered with chocolate sage. Wren dampened a paper towel with water from the sink and tried wiping it off. Her glittery gold face paint made her look unreal in all of the candlelight. The closer that she got to me, the more I could smell her flowery scent.

"There, that's better," Wren said as she tossed the paper towel onto the kitchen counter. "Come on, let's check out the balcony."

It was more than a balcony; in fact, I classified it as a straight-up patio.

As we approached the edge, it all came into

view—the hills below, the whole city, Berkeley's clock tower, and the bay beyond—all lit up by the descending sun. I was sure that I wouldn't want to live anywhere else.

An idea for a new poem suddenly came to me and all at once I knew what I would write about for my entry into the poetry contest at school. It would be called "The Second Part" and would be told from my point of view as a successful author, hosting my own book party like this one, living in a house like this one, being with a girl like Wren.

I turned to face her. The evening breeze had picked up and it caused her midnight-black hair to dance around her glittered face. I suddenly felt a surge of confidence that my recent inspiration had brought on.

Wren smiled up at me and inched closer. My heartbeat grew even louder to my ears and I tried to pretend that I was Jack Kerouac hanging out with one of the pretty girls that his characters always seemed to run into in his stories. Wren inched closer again.

I had to do it, I had to lean in and kiss her. So I took a deep breath, wrapped my arms around her, and did.

———

The next few days, at home and at school, sped by in a blur.

That Friday morning the rain poured down hard and it was the last thing I needed. I was late for school, I had neglected to take an umbrella with me, and I was trying and failing to keep my book bag dry. In it was a very precious item.

I was on my way to Ms. Reese's first period Lit class, where I would turn in my entry for the Junior Year Poetry Contest. I had worked constantly on the poem for the past week and I was certain that it was the best I had written yet. In the process, I had kind of pushed the work for my other courses to the side. I had asked my Government teacher if my presentation could be rescheduled, and I hadn't done my Trig homework in a few days. I was lucky that Mr. Kim only checked homework assignments weekly, meaning that he wouldn't expect any work turned in until next week. I would have to do it over the weekend.

Apart from Lit class every morning, and the Thursday Poetry Club meeting, I had seen Wren only once. After school on Wednesday we had gone to Weir's Weird Ice Cream Shop to share some actually-frozen Cedar Sage Chocolate. She loved it—as everyone in his or her right mind did—and we got to share the poems that we were working on with each other.

I had been surprised at how good Wren's was. I knew that she was talented at most things, and I was head over heels for her. I had even taken to snooping around her Facebook page, something I usually tried to avoid. Since the book party, I thought about her all the time. On Thursday I took her to meet

Bobcat the Bartender at Vesuvio, after the Poetry Club meeting. He served us ginger ales and told Wren all about the history of the place. I showed her the upstairs portion, with its cool black-and-white photographs and retro posters.

Wren read her poem to me and it was incredible, all about this magnolia tree in a garden somewhere in Georgia. When I asked her if she liked Georgia, she said that she had never been there before. I was amazed—but then again, my sci-fi story on the mer-people wasn't based on real events either.

I finished the last bit of my ginger ale as Wren read the last line of her poem. We were the only ones in the shop and she looked up at me.

"*Well*—what do you think? I'm going to enter it into the contest on Friday."

"I love it," I told her, because I really did.

Wren had liked my poem too, the one I had gotten the idea for at her dad's party. It was my way of creating my future, or at least how I wanted it to be—living in an awesome house in Berkeley with views of the city, publishing book after book of my own material and having celebratory book parties, and living with a joyful gorgeous girl who dug me and who I dug right back. I had typed the final copy last night at eleven o'clock after multiple versions, with Sal the Cat eyeing me suspiciously from his perch on the windowsill. I hadn't had much time to play with him lately because of my devotion to working on the poem, and he always got moody when that happened. I trusted that he would come back around.

The rain was still pouring down relentlessly as I got to school. I rushed in through the main entrance, threw my junk in my locker, and ran into Ms. Reese's classroom. Even though I was getting there nearly fifteen minutes late, it seemed that I hadn't missed much. Wren waved at me as I took my seat next to Tyler and Carmelita. Ms. Reese was still writing assignment dates and topic points up on the board.

"Hey, guys," I said as I dug through my bag for

the poem. Once I found it, I felt relieved to find it only slightly wet from the rain. "Where do I—"

"Right there," Tyler answered, pointing to a stack of papers on Ms. Reese's desk. I threw my poem in and sat back on my ottoman to take a moment and relax. I had worked hard on it and needed sleep desperately.

"Best of luck, my man," Tyler said.

"Thanks. How did your poems come out, you guys?"

"I felt sort of strained, man, I don't know," Tyler answered. "Ever since this poetry club stuff I think too much about the whole thing, you know? It's harder to ease into a brilliant idea now."

"Hmm, I think I get you, Tyler. What about it, Car?"

She looked over at me and deeply into my eyes. We hadn't seen each other that much lately, and I wasn't sure if she knew what had gone down between Wren and me last weekend. Carmelita had decided to walk to school alone this week, saying something about dropping packages off at the post office for her mom every morning, which would have taken us too far out of the way. But this was ridiculous; the post office never opened before nine.

Today Carmelita wore the denim skirt that made it difficult for me to concentrate on anything else whenever I glanced at her. She looked extra pretty—but probably because I hadn't seen her enough lately.

"Hunter?" Carmelita reached across Tyler and touched my arm to make sure that she had my attention. She did.

"Yeah?"

"Wait for me after last period okay? We can walk home together, maybe stop off at Weir's."

The way that she said it gave me a funny feeling in my stomach. What was going on?

"Sure thing, Car. I'll see you later."

———

It stopped raining at around three-thirty that afternoon, when the sun began to poke out from behind swarms of grey clouds.

"What do you want, Carmelita?"

We had just entered Weir's and taken a table near the back of the store. Car stared at me in disbelief.

"*Really?* What do I always order, Hunter?"

"One scoop of cedar sage chocolate, one scoop of cherry cardamom."

"Well there it is, that's what I want."

She laughed as I went up to the counter. Maybe Carmelita didn't notice anything different about us, but I did.

Since spending more time with Wren, I had become super aware of a girl and a guy being out together and what that might mean. Even though Car had been my close friend for years and we had been out together many times, it suddenly felt more significant. It almost felt like a date.

I brought back the orders to the table and Car reached into her wallet to pay me.

"Ah no—don't worry about it," I said.

"Hunter please, you do *not* have to pay for me," she responded, still digging around in her wallet.

"I know." My face felt hot again. "I want to."

"Okay, well . . . thanks."

We ate in silence for a few moments before Carmelita spoke again.

"Are you gonna see your girlfriend again this weekend?"

"Who, you mean Wren?"

"That's right."

"She's not my girlfriend, Car—"

"Well, whatever the heck she is—"

"Not my girlfriend, we're just . . . hanging out."

Carmelita furrowed her brow and seemed to go deep in thought.

"Right," she said, "but isn't that what we do? Just hang out?"

She looked up at me and seemed to suggest

something with her eyes that I didn't want to think about.

"Well, sure, I guess."

Car put her spoon down in a decided way and looked at me intensely again. I had seen her like this only once before—when she had told me about breaking up with her ex, the math tutor nerd Walter Preiner, in freshman year. And I had a feeling that I knew where she was headed with this, and I wasn't sure that I wanted to head there with her. I was going through a lot at the moment—with my writing, and Wren—and I didn't need this too.

"Look Hunter, I'm *sure* you know by now that I've been into you for a long time."

I nearly choked on my ice cream. "*What?*"

Car threw her head back and laughed. I couldn't imagine what was so funny; this felt like a very important moment.

"Oh come on, you've *always* known it! I've tried to hint at it, to feel you out over the past year after I realized how *I* felt, but you didn't pick it up."

"What do you mean, 'didn't pick it up'? Were you super *obvious* about it or something?"

Carmelita sighed and looked to either side of her, like she didn't want to have to explain further.

"I thought that I was . . . I don't know. I *do* know that we have a great friendship and I don't want to mess that up. And I know that you're into this crazy chick from class and that's fine. Even if we don't agree on everything, I don't want to lose you . . . you know, as my friend."

I felt a sudden flash of memory as I remembered Carmelita coming to my apartment during freshman year, weeping. She had torn me away from the girl I wanted at the time, torn me away from Mara. I remembered Car spending the night with me in my room, after she had told me all about Walter and the break-up. Us falling asleep on opposite sides of the bed in the outfits we had worn to school that day. Car running out in the morning. How empty my room had felt once she'd left.

I didn't know what to say. All of this was a lot

to take in. It annoyed me that Carmelita was acting like it was all over and done with, like *of course* I knew that she had feelings for me, and *of course* I had turned her down many times. When had all this happened, really? Where had I been?

"Well, it sounds like you've got it all figured out, then. Thanks for your blessing." My tone sounded harsher and more sarcastic than I had intended, but I was ticked off.

"Oh stop, Hunter. I've always had guy friends. I'm used to this happening. Just friends is fine."

I sighed in annoyance.

Why was she articulating all of this? Why was Carmelita bringing this up now, now that I had a romantic possibility with Wren?

Now Car wanted to tell me that *she* should be dating me instead? Even though she'd known me *for years* and could have brought the issue up *at any time*? She made everything messy and difficult. She made it sound like I had missed an opportunity of some great worth, which was total news to me.

Well, I wouldn't make this easy for her then. I *would* play dumb.

"Look, Car, frankly, I don't really know what you're talking about here."

She knew me too well and eyed me skeptically.

"Fine then, just forget I said anything."

"Okay, *great*."

Carmelita folded her arms across her chest in defiance and sighed.

"I've got to go, Hunter. I'm supposed to meet Julian to check out this concert in Oakland. His brother plays guitar in some rock band with a weird name—the Lemon Lennons or something."

Julian Frey, that *double-crossing*—so, he wanted Carmelita now.

"Julian, huh? Not so sure about him these days."

"You love Julian, Ziv—"

"I used to, but lately he seems uber-paranoid, don't you think?"

Carmelita laughed and stood up to leave.

"Whatever you say, Ziv. Have a great weekend.

Let's walk to school together again on Monday, okay?"

She smiled at me and I felt my cheeks get hot. I looked away fast, hoping that she hadn't noticed.

"Okay. You too." I stood up to hug her good-bye like I usually did. Suddenly I didn't want her to leave. Suddenly I didn't want to let her go. But I had to.

When I got home, Mom and Dad told me that Amelia had left a note for me.

"I put it on your desk, tiger," Mom called over her shoulder. She and Dad were cooking eggplant parmigiana for dinner, my and Sal's favorite. Luckily the ice cream hadn't destroyed my appetite.

"Thanks, Mom. When's dinner?"

"Fifteen minutes," Dad replied.

"I'll be there," I said as I hurried to my room to check out the note. I was pretty sure that Amelia had left me the log-in info for an online poetry anthology she had told me about, like, three months ago. She had told me it included one of my favorite

Jack Kerouac poems that hadn't been published in any book or poetry journal.

Sal rubbed up against my leg to greet me when I reached my room. I hadn't been spending enough time with him and made a mental note to play our favorite game of fetch at least twice this weekend with his favorite green ball.

"Hey buddy," I said as I scratched his neck. He purred in reply.

I threw my book bag down and looked over the note, which included Amelia's username and password for the anthology's webpage.

I logged into the site on my laptop and began to skim through the archival contents. Most of the poems were by unknown authors that I didn't recognize, but I clicked on this rare 1940s Kerouac poem, which I started to read on a new page. The bottom of the page offered suggestions of which poem to read next, and one caught my eye because of its familiar title.

"Magnolia Monday" by Gladys Larson, 1931. I

clicked on it and was taken to the poem's page. As I read, I couldn't believe the words I encountered on the screen. *No*, I thought to myself, *it couldn't be.* But it sure as anything looked like the poem that Wren had shown to me, the one that she had entered into the contest at Henley, the one that she told me she had written.

I went to my desk and rifled through the untidy stack of pages there until I found it. Wren had given me a copy of her poem to edit on Wednesday and I had written up some suggestions. I still had the copy.

There it was: "Flowers on a Friday," by Wren Cooper. I placed the paper next to the laptop screen, with the poem by Gladys Larson.

Identical. Word for word.

Before I knew it, Sunday night was upon me again. The weekend had gone by in a rainy whirlwind during which I had mostly just tried to catch up on my schoolwork. I had succeeded in that, at least, uncharacteristically finishing all of my assignments by four in the afternoon, leaving my Sunday evening totally free. I had written my weekly essay for Ms. Reese on Saturday morning at around eight, which if someone had told me I was going to do last week, I wouldn't have believed him. Usually I slept until ten or eleven on weekend mornings—but in light of recent events I hadn't been sleeping well at all.

I wasn't sure what to do about Wren and the fact that she most likely had stolen that magnolia poem and claimed it as her own to submit into the contest. I kept thinking that there must be some explanation, but every time my mind followed a train of logical reasoning, it ran hard up against a brick wall of high improbability.

For instance: perhaps Wren really had authored the poem and published it under the penname Gladys Larson . . . in 1931, because she had access to a time machine and got her kicks from being published in different historical eras . . . No, not likely.

Perhaps Wren had promised Gladys on her deathbed that she would make sure that her magnolia poem was appreciated by modern audiences too, vowing to get it published again under a new name . . . But when I googled Larson I discovered that she had died in 1988 before Wren was even born . . . No, not likely.

Perhaps Amelia's poetry anthology webpage was a fake site full of stolen poems with fake years on them. Maybe someone *using* the name Gladys Larson was a plagiarizer herself—and had used Larson's name and stolen the poem from *Wren* and Wren didn't even know . . . No, not likely.

With all of these scenarios running through my mind, I hardly slept a wink.

I just couldn't imagine Wren blatantly stealing someone's idea; I couldn't imagine anyone doing it, really. As a writer myself, it would be my worst *nightmare* to see something I had written and which had come from my own unique mind, claimed by someone else too cowardly to do his or her own work. Wren didn't seem cowardly but instead seemed just the opposite. All of her positivity, her enthusiasm about the poetry club, her interest in the history of North Beach and the Beats, her seeming belief in the "First thought, best thought" philosophy—could these qualities point to Wren being a thief and liar?

Wren and I had made plans to go to Sausalito on Saturday but I suggested we reschedule, using the bad weather as an excuse. The truth was that I wasn't ready to see her just yet, not until I figured out how to approach her about my discovery. I didn't want to *accuse* her of anything necessarily, but I did want to know the real story, especially since she had entered the poem into the contest. What if she ended up winning? If the poem had been published before, it stood a good chance at being published again!

I paced around my room, which suddenly felt very small and prisonlike. Sal eyed me suspiciously from his perch on the bookshelf. I picked him up and put him on my shoulders, his purring growing louder. From my window, I watched the green trees outside get whipped about by the pounding rain. My brain felt like one of them.

I put Sal down and walked toward the study.

Mom had taken one of her classes to an evening seminar, but Dad was home and working on a new research paper. I found him hunched over his desk surrounded by books of all shapes and sizes. I needed to talk to him.

"Dad?"

He jumped about a foot in the air and then breathed a sigh of relief when he saw me.

"You scared me, Hunter, sorry. I've been miles away in this research for the past hour. What's going on? I should probably make us some dinner soon. It's after seven and Mom won't be home until later."

"Nah, that's okay. I'm not too hungry," I replied, taking a seat in Mom's rocking chair.

Dad took off his glasses, rubbed his eyes, and spun around in his desk chair to face me.

"All right. Hey Hunt, anything wrong? You seem like there's something bothering you."

Was it that obvious?

"Can I ask you something, Dad? Can I ask you

what you would do in a situation—a theoretical situation?"

"Sure. Ask away."

"What would you do if you thought that somebody was stealing someone else's work?"

Dad raised his eyebrows. "Stealing?"

"Well yeah, taking something that someone else had written and putting his—or her—own name on it instead. Plagiarizing, I guess is the *official* name for it."

"Hunter, you know how Mom and I feel about plagiarism, how the university holds plagiarism as one of the worst student crimes possible."

I didn't want Dad to get too heavy-handed about all this. Couldn't he be neutral for like, five minutes?

"I know but—" I began to answer.

"Creativity is one of the highest values that we . . . I mean, it is to be respected and credited accurately—"

Dad was getting all worked up, I could tell. He

had taken off his glasses, and the pace of his speech increased.

"Right, but Dad, what if by republishing the piece—well, what if it was the only option? What if the—the—stealer-writer had run out of time by a deadline, you know?"

Dad thought about it some more, then shook his head.

"Think about it this way. How would you feel if you found one of your pieces claimed by someone else, even though you had written it?"

I thought seriously before I answered.

"Well, if it happened to be a cultural manifesto that was going to change the world, I'd have to put my ego aside and just be glad that it was out there in the world. Anything other than that, well, I'd be super, super angry."

"Of course you would, and you would have a right to be. Plagiarizing is stealing, Hunter. It's never good."

I got a creepy feeling in my stomach when he said it. I had been thinking the same thing.

———

The next morning I waited outside on the lawn for Carmelita. The grass was still drenched from the weekend of rain, but the Monday sun shone brightly up above. I chose to believe that it was a good omen.

I hadn't seen Car since Friday at Weir's, and I felt a bit nervous about seeing her again. Would things be different between us now? She had acted like they wouldn't, but I wasn't so sure. I had been a bit preoccupied with the whole Wren-as-Gladys-Larson debacle all weekend and had put off processing what Carmelita had told me. But this morning it stared me in the face once more. It didn't help that I had dreamt about her again last night.

In the dream, she had started out as Wren before

morphing into Carmelita, who repeated the speech that she had fed to me on Friday. In the dream, it led into a confession of being in love with Tyler.

I suppose it was more of a nightmare than a dream.

I turned to see Carmelita running down the stairs in her favorite converse and a flower print dress.

"Sorry, Ziv! I'm coming!"

She had almost reached me when she stumbled over a rogue tree root on the lawn and fell, her books flying everywhere. I ran to help her up.

"Car—Car, are you all right?"

She took my hand and tried to stand up but then tripped again on her dress. She burst out laughing and couldn't seem to stop.

"I'm . . . *fine*," she said between laughs. "Happy to have started the week off on the right foot."

That got me going, too, and soon neither of us could stop laughing. Finally, she stood up and looked me square in the face.

"Hey," she said, smiling.

"Hey, yourself."

Her eyes looked clearer, her gaze more direct. I felt like it was the first time that I had ever looked at her.

"*Well?*" she replied.

"Well, what?"

Did she want me to kiss her or something?

"Well, don't you think we should get going if we don't want to miss the announcement about the contest?"

"Oh, right."

Suddenly I wished the whole contest-and-poetry-club-thing had never even happened.

We walked along the road in the direction of Henley High.

"Have you planned on what your concession speech will be when you . . . *lose* to me?" Carmelita joked.

"Ha *ha*. That'll never happen."

"Famous last words!"

It really was a beautiful morning. We even

spotted a few butterflies hanging around the tulip garden that was outside Weir's.

"How was the concert?" I asked, trying to sound only half-interested.

"Oh man, it was great! Julian's brother was a total whacko! He spent most of the concert crowd surfing. Eventually he threw away his mic and just surfed while the band jammed."

"I'm not surprised, I guess. Sounded like a make-shift operation."

"Oh sure, but it was a lot of fun."

I felt all tight inside. I suddenly remembered my nightmare from last night, and how Tyler and Car had walked off together, super into each other, and away from me.

"Julian didn't try anything on you, did he?"

"What do you mean?"

"He wasn't . . . all over you . . . or anything?"

I was pretty sure that I sounded like a nut but I couldn't stop myself. Carmelita started laughing again.

"Julian? I don't even think he likes girls! What is going on with you, Hunter?"

A lot, Car, a real lot. Suddenly the idea of you with any guy other than me makes me feel sick.

"What about Tyler?"

I had gone too far. Carmelita stopped dead in her tracks even though we were just one block away from school. Groups of students passed us by. Some stopped to look and then kept walking. Car took my hand and pulled us over and out of the way.

"Look," she said, "I missed you at the concert on Friday night. *I want us to be friends,* okay? I'm really sorry if . . . if I freaked you out on Friday when I told you, you know, how I feel. Felt."

The correction of tense intrigued me. She went on.

"I probably shouldn't've told you because it doesn't matter anymore; you've got someone else, anyway. You've been so serious lately. Maybe we both have. You know, you *can* be a great writer and still have fun."

"Car?"

We had started walking again, toward the main doors of Henley.

"What would you do if you thought that somebody was stealing someone else's work?"

She stopped short again and sighed, exasperated with me. "What?"

"If you thought that someone had stolen someone else's work and put his own name on it instead?"

Carmelita scanned my face carefully, trying to read it.

"Thought or knew?"

"Thought, I think."

Carmelita walked over to the lockers and I followed. She hastily threw her Physics book in and shut the door to relock it.

"I would ask him how it felt to steal other people's hard-earned intellectual property. I would tell him to get a life," she said over her shoulder as she walked toward Ms. Reese's room. "You coming?"

That settled it for me.

When I reached Ms. Reese's classroom, I took my seat with Car and Tyler. I felt kind of relieved to see them in real life and not . . . declaring any wild love for each other. It seemed that some kind of spell had broken. Suddenly the idea of Wren turned me off immensely. I really did *not* want to see her and hoped that she would be absent. Something told me she wouldn't be though. Ms. Reese was going to announce the three finalists of the poetry contest today, and I was sure that Wren would want to hear the results.

Just like that, there she was. Wren waltzed in and took her usual seat on the other side of the room. She looked beautiful in a black dress and black ballet slippers. When she saw me, she gave a soft wave and mouthed a *Hi*! I was suddenly extra aware of myself and of Wren, and I didn't want anybody to get the wrong idea about us. I didn't want them to think that we were together or anything; I didn't want Carmelita to think so in any case. I smiled back at

Wren in an attempt to seem friendly and felt my cheeks burn in embarrassment. How perfect. If I were writing the short story, I would've written it just this way too:

Hunter Zivotovsky, writer-genius extraordinaire, finally got the girl he'd always wanted . . . only to realize that he didn't want her at all. And that she might be the biggest plagiarizer of all time . . .

Oh boy, that part *nauseated* me. If Wren really did steal the poem, and Ms. Reese or the Dandicat Press people found out, would she be arrested? Wouldn't legal stuff come into play, like copyright issues? I was starting to think that I was in over my head.

Ms. Reese came striding into the classroom and I felt relieved at once. If anyone would be able to straighten all of this out, it would be her.

"Good morning, everybody. Good weekends, despite the three-day-long raging monsoon?"

There was an assortment of half-hearted responses throughout the room.

"Glad to hear it. Pass your essays forward, if you please. Then I'll get to the exciting news that I'm sure you're anxiously waiting to hear."

I dug my paper out of my bag, which I had typed—and saved, multiple times—on my laptop. These days it was difficult to know when someone might decide to tear up a writer's only copy at random.

Once she had collected everyone's work, Ms. Reese stood in the center of the room holding a piece of official-looking paper.

"Here in my hands, I hold the results of Dandicat Press's decisions on the contest finalists! Is everybody ready?"

Most of the class had woken up by now and sat in focused attention, awaiting the news. Only Julian Frey was still dozing off as he usually did on Monday mornings. Kate Shankar kept nudging him in the ribs to wake him up.

"Oh, and," Ms. Reese added, "the contest judges provided comments on each poem that was submitted. So even if you didn't advance to the semi-finals, you will still receive highly valuable feedback from some very insightful editors. Sound good?"

There were some nods and grunts of agreement.

"Next week you guys, I am bringing coffee in for everyone, okay? Because *this does not cut it* . . . Okay. The three finalists of the contest are . . . "

My heart thumped loudly in my chest. The future of my literary career hung in the balance—maybe.

"Carmelita Lorca, Kate Shankar, and Wren Cooper!"

The room burst into applause. I had to remind myself to join in.

Truth be told, I was in a state of semi-shock that my poem hadn't made it. I was borderline in a state of panic too that Wren's—or Gladys Larson's— poem *had* made it. What if she won? Would that be fair to the real Gladys, to Ms. Reese and the Dandicat Press judges, to Kate and—Carmelita?

I would ask him how it felt to steal other people's hard-earned intellectual property. I would tell him to get a life.

I looked over at Car, whom Tyler and Julian were congratulating and saying encouraging words to.

"Congrats, Car. I'm . . . well, I'm proud of you," I told her loudly over the many conversations going on all over the room.

"Thanks, Ziv," she replied, beaming at me.

I felt surer than ever that I liked Carmelita, that I liked her as more than a friend. The timing of this was terrible. It was all too much. Son of a—

"Hunter?"

Ms. Reese was standing above me with a stack of papers in her hands. She handed my poem back to me.

"Well done, Hunter. The editors said that you nearly made it to the semifinals. Keep up the good work. Be sure to read the comments on the back too, I think they'll help you."

"Thanks, Ms. Reese."

I looked through my poem and felt a mixture of contempt and love for it. I had truly believed that I was going to win.

On the back of the paper were a few handwritten comments made by the editor judges.

Excellent, clear voice and style. Confidence evident. Word usage impressive for grade level. Shows artistic promise. Overly serious in subject and tone, which lessens the emotional effect of the poem.

This last bit sounded especially familiar. I looked over at Carmelita, who was laughing with Tyler.

You've been so serious lately. You know, you can be a great writer and still have fun.

Right again, Carmelita, I thought to myself. *You always are.*

9

Maybe what I thought I had wanted, I didn't really want after all.

I knew that I wanted to be a writer. I knew that I loved Jack Kerouac and the other Beat poets and their writing. When Wren and her dumbo sidekick Will came along with the poetry club, and then when the poetry contest happened, I must've gotten caught up in all of it.

I had been crushing on Wren for months—since I had run into her at the library, right after she moved to Berkeley. When she singled out my poem and then invited me to her dad's book party, it was like seeing my dream realized in a matter of weeks. It was all so perfect, even Wren.

But what if perfection didn't exist? A poem about perfection then, like my contest entry, could seem creepy, fake, boring—and *overly serious*.

What if Wren really was a plagiarizer, or at the very least what if she had been involved in—*antics that were questionable*, as far as the authenticity of her poem went? It made me want to reconsider everything that had gone down these past few weeks.

Mr. Cooper's book party. Yes, it had been an incredibly cool event at an incredibly cool house attended by incredibly cool guests. Yes, Mr. Cooper wore incredibly cool glasses. But something had bothered me about the way he had reacted to the ice cream situation. It was true that I had goofed by forgetting to give it to Wren right away, but people goof up sometimes. It had been nice of me to bring something to the party. Wasn't it super *un*cool to get uptight on me the way that he did?

The first poetry club meeting. Yes, it had been

full of theatrics that had been exciting and a bit shocking and seemed like something that the Beats might have been into. Yes, I had been proud of myself for writing a really good poem on the spot after the other one I wrote had been destroyed. Yes, I had enjoyed being singled out for my work, in front of the others and especially Wren. But something had bothered me about Will and how he'd jumped on Carmelita's abilities the way that he did. Wasn't it *so* not in line with the Beats' attitude of freedom and acceptance?

My longtime pals Tyler, Julian, and Carmelita. All of them had at one point or another expressed concern over getting involved in the club. Not that I made a habit out of caring too much about others' opinions, but these weren't just "others," they were friends who knew me well and who I trusted. I had let my ego get the better of me and assumed that my friends' reservations were just them being jealous of my success. Then I became a bewildered control freak, ruled by the fear that Carmelita would get close to another guy, closer than she was with me. It doesn't get any more uncool than that!

My coursework. I'd been neglecting it for nearly all of my other classes. I'd felt it didn't apply to me because I only cared about writing. I did care about writing most, but I was still in school after all—*high school*—I'd have to apply to college next year. I'd have to take the SATs in a few months!

I wasn't off the hook. The awesome house, book party, friends, were all great—but they had to be mine, right? They had to be . . . *authentic*. I didn't want to plagiarize a dream life, to take someone else's that was already successful, stick my name on it, and hope that nobody found out. I didn't want to do something like Wren had probably done.

My contest entry poem had described how I wanted my adult life to be. Since the poem hadn't made it into the next round, I almost felt like the ideas in it hadn't either. It wasn't just my poem that had been judged, it was all of my plans for the future, too.

That same night, Monday, after Ms. Reese had made the semifinal announcements, I was supposed to go to Sausalito with Wren, making up for the date we had missed over the weekend. I texted her after school and asked if we could meet at Weir's Weird Ice Cream Shop instead. I didn't have time to go all the way to Sausalito on a school night, not with the catching up I had to do on my homework. Plus, I wanted to be in a comfortable and familiar environment when I asked Wren some questions about "Flowers on a Friday" or whatever it was called.

I got to Weir's around six and Wren was already there. She sat at a table by herself, typing something on her phone. Her face looked tired and devoid of emotion. It was strange to see her without an overwhelming grin. I wondered whether she had always looked kind of unhappy and I just hadn't noticed it until now.

I walked into Weir's as the door entry bell jingle announced my arrival. Wren turned to see who it was and instantly smiled when she saw me. I went to her and she stood to greet me, kissing me on the cheek and hugging me tightly. I still had feelings for her; maybe I always would. But I wished that she would let me go.

"Did you order yet?" I asked her.

"No, I wanted to wait for you. I'd love some of that stellar flavor that you brought to the party! I forgot my wallet at home though."

She made an over-the-top sad face as she said this, in an attempt to be cute, I thought. I felt like I couldn't trust her now. Was she trying to manipulate me? Had she always been?

"It's okay, I got it."

I walked up to the counter, about to order two of the same. *No*, I thought to myself. *Time to change it up.*

"One cup of cedar sage chocolate, and one cup of raspberry thyme, please."

I paid using the last of the month's allowance—I had been spending too much money evidently, as it was only the nineteenth of October—and brought the cups to our table.

"Thanks, Hunter!" Wren said enthusiastically as she dug into her ice cream. "Wow, this is the best, *ab-so-lute-ly*."

I didn't have much of an appetite but attempted to make some headway on the raspberry thyme, my second favorite flavor at Weir's. I was trying to figure out the best way to ask about the source of Wren's poem without insulting her.

"I guess this is really a celebratory dessert, isn't it, Hunter?" she asked.

"Oh yeah, the contest. Um . . . congratulations! Do you think you'll win?"

"I *think* so—I mean, probably. Based on the work that I've seen so far of the other semi-finalists, anyway. Wow, publication! I am *ex-ciiiited*."

How to go about this? I could ask about her inspiration for "Flowers on a Friday." I stuffed a huge scoop of raspberry thyme into my mouth and got an instant and intense ice cream headache.

"Well, Carmelita's work has always been pretty consistent," I said. "I'm not surprised that she made it at all."

Wren looked simultaneously annoyed and nervous.

"Oh yeah, well, I know you guys are friends. She's okay, I guess. The poem she turned in to Will at the club meeting though," she said, making a disgusted face, "was *wayyyyy* too angry. A turn-off, you know? Not like yours. Yours was . . . positive."

You mean it was about you? I thought to myself.

She had finished her ice cream and reached across the table to take my hand. I left it there for a second but then took it away, pretending that I had to scratch my shoulder. I didn't want my feelings for Wren, murky as they were at the moment, to get in the way of finding out what I needed to find out.

"Thanks. Well, at least Carmelita's was probably original, authentic. True—even if it was angry."

I looked down at my ice cream and took another big scoop. Frozen brain, again. Wren watched me in seeming curiosity before she tried to change the subject.

"Hunter, you still have to take me to Sausalito! I've been wanting to go since we moved here. How about this weekend? What's the best way to get there from Berkeley?"

I was finding it difficult to come to the point, the point that I wanted to make. The question that I wanted to ask Wren. Maybe I was being paranoid about this too, maybe she *had* written the poem. It was possible, wasn't it? Then, what would I do about Carmelita? Ignore what I felt, and stay with Wren?

What would I do about Carmelita either way?

"The BART's best," I answered. "The BART to the city and then the ferry from Fisherman's Wharf." I cleared my throat. "Wren—"

She looked up at me, straight-on, and I found it difficult to ask what I wanted to ask.

"—do you want more ice cream?" I started.

"No, that's okay, thanks. I've had enough."

Good thing too, because I was plain out of funds at the moment. I'd have to get to it.

"So Wren, how did you get the idea for your poem, the 'Flowers' one? It was really fantastic I thought, almost—like it was written in another time. Like, decades earlier."

She smiled, seeming to be flattered.

"Well you know that I absolutely love flowers. All kinds. I write about them a lot. This idea, this poem, it just sort of came to me, you know?"

I was still suspicious and didn't say anything but tried to appear nonchalant. She continued.

"First thought, best thought! Like the Beats went for, like the club goes for! Don't overthink it, just trust your inspiration."

As long as it's yours, I thought. Maybe it was best to come right out and say it. Maybe it was just a misunderstanding. Maybe we'd be laughing about the whole thing in two minutes.

"Right. Of course. Wren, have you . . . have you

ever read any 1930s poetry? Do you like that sort of thing?"

She looked into my eyes and then furrowed her brow.

"I guess so, sure . . . I like most poetry I read."

"Ever read anything by Larson? Gladys Larson?"

She had been playing with her ice cream spoon and dropped it on the first "Larson." It seemed that she had heard of her before.

"Who?"

"Larson. Gladys Larson. She wrote a poem called 'Magnolia Monday?' It's kind of obscure now, not taught in schools or anything, I don't think."

Wren looked terrified, like the wind could no longer hold up her sails.

"Hunter . . . Hunter, I . . . " She paused and took a deep breath. "I'm sorry. I can explain everything."

Even though I had been pretty sure that this was going to happen, even though my major shock had been when I found the Larson poem on the internet, I was still saddened by Wren's admittance. A small part of me somewhere inside had wanted to be wrong. A part of me wanted to go on liking Wren, to go on dating her. It was such a funny thing, too. I could still *feel* my crush on her—it hadn't disappeared! It just seemed impossible now, impossible for us to go any further. Which made me feel incredibly sad.

"See, Hunter, Will and I became hardcore poetry fans over the last few months," Wren said. "We read constantly, all of the poetry that we could get our hands on. He was the first friend that I made here in Berkeley. I didn't know too much about poetry before, only the basics, the greatest hits. Shakespeare, Keats, Dickinson, Frost, that sort of thing. We would take anthologies out of the university library and spend the weekends reading them straight through. This was about a month and a half ago, around the time that we got the idea to start a poetry club at school. Will's mom was friends with Ms. Reese and she was super into the idea when we told her. And the more that I read, the more that I wanted to *wow* people with my stuff."

I thought of myself suddenly, how I had wanted to do the same thing with my poem.

"My dad, too. You met him at the party. He's . . . well he's got high standards for writing. I have them too. And I ran out of time with all of my other assignments."

Wren spoke faster and faster and her eyes darted every which way. She was even breathing faster. I thought back to my first moments with her. I thought back to first seeing her outside the campus library that day. She had seemed like the most care-free girl in the world, a hippie princess. Now, Wren was a nervous wreck.

"The night before the contest entries were due," Wren continued, "I tried my best to pull something together. I was pretty happy with something I had written, and then I showed it to my dad . . . and I could tell that he didn't think it was any good. I could just . . . *tell.* And then it was *one in the morning*, Hunter, and I panicked. That's when it happened."

Wren had tears in her eyes, and it surprised me how scared she still was. I *knew* I had gotten bad vibes from Mr. Cooper, and having him as a dad . . . Well, I could see how he could freak Wren out about writing in general.

"What about Will? Was he in on this?"

"No, he . . . he doesn't know," she answered. Then she turned sharply toward me. "Don't tell him, okay? I just . . . I ran out of time! I did it with a Global Studies paper once, too, back in LA—"

"A paper? You mean you took one from the internet?"

I was feeling extremely tired out from this by now; the story seemed to be getting worse. Still, I felt badly for Wren.

"Just once, it was a while ago now."

I sat and stared down at my melted cup of raspberry thyme. For all of my presuming and planning, I didn't really know what to say now. I more or less understood Wren's larger issue. I understood what it felt like to be pressed for time on assignments. I spent most of my time working on schoolwork and my writing. But Wren had still plagiarized someone's poem. That had been optional, too. I mean, if Wren had really run out of time, she should've skipped submitting an entry into the contest. It hadn't been required by Ms. Reese. Wren's outlook was wrong . . . wasn't it?

"Wren . . . I mean . . . I just don't know. To me, it still seems . . . "

She sat up straight and focused her attention on me, interrupting.

"I think that Gladys Larson and these . . . these old *nobodies* would want their work out there for the world too, you know? I mean, it's not all bad!"

This was getting ridiculous.

"Well . . . maybe?" I answered, trying to stay calm. I felt like I had to stand up for old nobodies everywhere. "It's still wrong though. I mean, you're lying, putting your name on material that isn't yours! You're misleading your readers. Don't you see the . . . the immorality there?"

My voice had grown louder and the other people in Weir's were eyeing us curiously. I had gone too far. I seemed to be doing that a lot lately. Or maybe I was just being myself. Maybe I was tired of trying to be so cool all of the time. Maybe my face turned red when I got embarrassed. Maybe I was human.

Wren had folded her arms across her chest while I was ranting. She seemed to be very angry.

"Would you please . . . get out of here, Hunter? Just go. Leave me alone."

I stood up slowly. I didn't want to just leave her there.

"And don't text me ever again," she added.

"Wren, come on. Maybe . . . maybe I can help you. Help you figure out what to do, how to talk to Ms. Reese."

I touched Wren softly on the shoulder, trying to comfort her. I had tears in my eyes now, too. Was the only answer to never see each other again? She was still sure that she was right?

"I don't need your help, okay?" she insisted. "If you're the only one who knows, maybe I won't even have to talk to Ms. Reese at all."

"But what if you win?"

"Well, then I'd figure out what to do about it. You won't tell, Hunter—promise? If my dad found out, I don't think he'd ever forgive me!"

Wren grabbed my hand and held it as she looked into my eyes, pleading.

"You won't tell Will, right?" she went on.

I suddenly felt really badly for Wren. She didn't get it.

"No," I replied as I opened the door, "I won't tell anyone."

I hurried out of there and walked as fast as I could down University Avenue toward home. I popped my jacket collar to deflect the chill of the October night air, with the worst of tastes in my mouth.

I wouldn't tell anyone; I wasn't a snitch. The winner would be announced the next day. I just hoped that Wren wasn't it. I didn't think my conscience could let that slide. Especially when Carmelita was involved.

"Now, is everyone ready? I have the results here in my hands, straight from the Dandicat Press editors."

Ms. Reese sat in her director's chair, the kind that belonged on a movie set, at the front of the classroom. She opened a sealed manila envelope, slowly and deliberately, as our whole class watched in silence. Carmelita drummed her fingertips along the notebook in her lap, faster and faster. Kate Shankar clicked her jaw every three seconds in a steady and reliable rhythm. Wren was nowhere in sight.

"I'd like to congratulate everyone who submitted entries into the contest," Ms. Reese went on. "The editors at Dandicat Press told me how impressed they were with all of the poems from you guys. I'm excited to spend the rest of the academic year together. Even *with* the SAT prep coming up soon."

Everyone, including me, groaned at that last bit. Ms. Reese put her hands up in defense.

"All right everybody, that's enough."

Suddenly her manner and tone grew more serious and official. She put the envelope to the side for a moment.

"I'd also like to point out some unfortunate business that has come up in relation to the contest."

Ms. Reese paused, apparently searching for the right words. She had the whole class's attention now. I had a funny sensation in my stomach again. Ms. Reese took a deep breath and continued.

"One of the Dandicat editors discovered that one of the contest entry poems was less than original. It was proven to have been plagiarized from an alternate source."

Expressions of shock and surprise rose up from everyone except me. I *was* taken aback by how fast Ms. Reese and the Dandicat editors had found out. Relief swept over me too, knowing that I wouldn't have to decide whether or not to turn Wren in for plagiarism. I wished I could've explained to her myself that . . . well, that I'd rather turn in the worst poem I'd ever written than anything of someone else's. Because at the end of the day, it was just a dumb high school contest! I mean, it didn't matter that much in the big scheme of things!

"Apparently," Ms. Reese continued, "the poet from whom the student took the poem happened to be an old mentor of one of the contest judges who recognized the work instantly. Interesting, too, given that the poem is so obscure. I had never heard of it before myself. So as is fitting, the entry poem has been dismissed from the contest."

I heard Wren's name mentioned here and there

amidst the chatter in the room. Carmelita and Tyler both shot me looks of concern. Tyler made a disappointed face, while Car mouthed, *You okay?* I nodded that I was. Ms. Reese stood up from her director's chair and paced around the room a bit as she continued to talk.

"I'd also like to say to you guys now, that you should never feel that you have to resort to stealing if you either can't come up with a creative idea or for some reason can't finish an assignment. Authenticity is the best and most powerful quality that you as writers can bring to creative work. It is what makes you, *you*. And it's irreplaceable. Have confidence enough to know that."

The class was still quiet and attentive as Ms. Reese took a deep breath and reached for the results envelope once more.

"Now, onto bigger and better, brighter, and most of all lighter, things. Let's do this. The winner of the poetry contest is . . . Carmelita Lorca!"

The room erupted into applause. Kate Shankar

looked vaguely disappointed but congratulated Car just the same. I was so proud of Carmelita. She was always direct, straight with me, honest, smarter than me. She was onto Will and the club's ridiculousness one minute into the first meeting. Before *that* even.

"Congratulations, Carmelita. We look forward to reading the next issue of the *Dandicat Press Literary Journal*, with your poem inside it, the only one by a high school student. Most excellent."

"Thank you, Ms. Reese," Car said, beaming.

She looked extraordinarily happy. She looked beautiful. She was the coolest girl that I had ever met, and she was my best friend.

"Great job, Car," I said. "You deserve it."

"Thanks, Hunt."

I suddenly had the desperate urge to speak with her, alone. I felt like I had all of this stuff to tell her. We hadn't talked—*really* talked—in so long. Now she was getting her work published in a real literary journal. I didn't want her to forget about me.

I've tried to hint at it, to feel you out over the past

year after I realized how I felt, but you didn't pick it up.

Zivotovsky, you fool!

Just friends is fine . . .

"Car?" I asked. "What are you doing for lunch? Maybe we could—"

Everybody was trying to talk to Carmelita at once. We were a bunch of Honors Lit nerds after all—what had I expected? It was a big deal. Ms. Reese had sat back down in her chair and seemed to be grading our recent essays, having given up on trying to get us focused.

Car heard me.

"Sorry, Ziv, I have to go to Physics tutoring during lunch today. The future of my academic life depends on it, otherwise I would skip."

She smiled at me warmly, but I was worried. I didn't want to lose her.

The rest of the day dragged on. I saw Carmelita twice more throughout the rest of classes, but both times she had been with someone who was dragging her off somewhere. I couldn't seem to be with her for longer than thirty seconds. It was an important day for her, for her literary career, something that we had talked about and planned for often. Perfect. After spending years as her right-hand man, clocking hours and hours of hangout time—after living in the same building—I couldn't get close to her today, when I really needed to. When I really wanted her badly.

By the end of the day I felt strung out on her. It seemed like the longest Tuesday in history. I had a near miss in Trig when Mr. Kim called on me to answer a question I hadn't even heard asked. I couldn't concentrate on anything other than talking to Carmelita as soon as possible.

I chose to wait for her outside by the exit doors after tenth period. We usually walked home together anyway, but since I hadn't spoken to her all day, I was worried about whether our routine would carry through as usual. Now Carmelita was a published author. I remembered how I had changed when I was singled out in the poetry club. She was liable to change at any minute.

But she didn't. At three thirty sharp, roughly ten or so minutes after most Henley students had fled for the day, Car came trotting down the main stairs. I had seen her perform this same action so many times before, but today it seemed different. I wanted something from her today, I guessed. Something more.

"Hunter! Am I glad to see *you*. Today has been *craaaaazy*," she said as she walked toward me. She walked purposefully slow for comedic effect.

"Well you're a bigwig published writer, now. Contest-winner too. Quite a day for you, Car."

She threw her head back and laughed. The sun shone strongly above us as Car put on her aviator shades. We started to walk toward home. A few blocks passed before I could muster up the courage to tell Carmelita what I needed to. To tell her in just the right way.

"Yeah, well. I better get used to it, right? *You* better get used to it too, Ziv."

"Huh?"

"You're going to be a published author too. Anyone with half a brain knows that."

"Thanks, Car."

"Really. I was pretty sure you would have made it to the semifinal round."

"Thanks, but I wasn't surprised. The poem that I turned in . . . well let's just say, it wasn't like *me*. It was more like what I was trying to be."

We walked along in silence for a bit. This courage-mustering was harder than I thought. But if Carmelita could do it with her confession at Weir's last Friday, so could I.

I reached out and took her hand. It was easier than I thought it would be. She didn't pull away, and we stayed like that for a while. The afternoon breeze blew at its own whims. *Here goes*, I thought.

"Carmelita, I want to talk to you about something."

"Okay."

"About the other night. About Friday."

Car squeezed my hand. "Hunt, I told you—"

"No, I know, I know. But *I* didn't tell *you*, you know? I didn't really tell you what I thought."

We passed Weir's Weird Ice Cream Shop and I got a flash craving for Raspberry Thyme. Wow, I really *was* changing. Cedar sage chocolate was the furthest thing from my mind. I liked the way that Carmelita's hand felt in mine. It felt obvious. It felt right.

"Carmelita, I'm sorry for being a dumb . . . well, a dumb person. I didn't see a lot of things that were true. I didn't see you, not really. I mean, I didn't see how I really felt about you. This whole poetry contest and everything surrounding it . . . I just wanted to apologize to you, for not really being here lately. I've been off in my own world."

"Yeah well, we all do that sometimes, Ziv. I

mean, you were working on stuff. It's okay. You're supposed to."

"No, Car, you're not listening to me. You're being too . . . too *nice*. I'm trying to tell you something here."

"Okay, well then tell me."

I stopped abruptly on the sidewalk. There was a cluster of trees off behind the bakery on Telegraph Avenue and we walked over to it.

"Car, I'm sorry for neglecting you."

She leaned against a tree and burst out laughing.

"What are you *talking* about, Hunter?"

"I'm sorry for not seeing the truth about you sooner. The truth about, you know, us."

She grew serious again and looked me straight in the eye. I felt my cheeks get red again but I didn't care.

"The truth?" she asked.

"Yeah," I tried to explain, "you know what it is. You said it on Friday."

She raised an eyebrow.

"But I'm nervous now," I went on. Carmelita looked confused.

"Nervous?"

I put my hands in my pockets and walked a step or two away and then back, thinking.

"Well yeah, nervous. I mean last *I* heard, just friends was fine. Your words, Carmelita. But you see, it's not *really* fine. Not with me. What about more? What about . . . more than just friends?"

She stared at me for a moment but didn't speak, like she was waiting for me to go on with my speech. Maybe I hadn't been courageous enough.

"Carmelita, things have changed here, all right? They're different now."

I put my hands on her shoulders and looked her straight in the eyes.

"I want you now," I went on. "Do you still want me?"

She looked at me for a moment and I wasn't sure what she would do. Then she suddenly pulled me toward her and the tree that she leaned against. We kissed.

That was that.

———

"Look at this, Carmelita."

"What is it?"

"It's your work, on sale here in City Lights. Living the dream—literally."

I picked up the copy of *Dandicat Press Literary Journal* and flipped to the page with Carmelita's winning poem on it. I pointed to it and smiled.

"There it is. Genius realized. There you are."

Car laughed. "Can I keep you around? Good for my ego, you know?"

I looked over each shoulder, making sure there was no one around the bookshelf aisle that we currently occupied.

I leaned in and kissed her.

"Ahem," someone said in a purposefully

pronounced way. It was Tyler. Carmelita and I looked up, caught. We'd been together for a month but hadn't made it official. It hadn't been announced on Facebook yet.

"It's about time," Tyler said smiling. Car and I looked over. I was pretty sure that I'd turned red upon being discovered. I didn't care though.

"Have you seen this?" I asked Tyler, grabbing the copy of *Dandicat Press Literary Journal* from the shelf. Tyler smiled and nodded.

"That I have, my man. Congratulations Car, it's now official."

"Thanks, Tyler," she replied.

Suddenly Tyler's face lit up. He had remembered something important.

"Hey! Guess who I ran into on the way over?"

"Ms. Reese?" I asked.

"Nah," Tyler answered, "Will. He mentioned the poetry club."

"Really? What'd he say?" Carmelita asked.

"Well," Tyler began, leafing through a copy

of Flannery O'Connor stories. "Apparently, The Henley High Poetry Club has gone on hiatus."

"Hopefully a permanent one," Carmelita said, taking my hand.

"It sounded like it might be that kind of a thing," Tyler went on.

I had seen Wren a few times around Berkeley over the past few weeks. She had been suspended from Henley High for plagiarism; she'd been caught for stealing a few of her other assignments that she had turned in last month, too. Whenever Wren saw me she became instantly paranoid and started walking the other way. It was awful. I wished that we could still be friends or something. I didn't think it was evil, what she had done, just . . . totally wrong and uncool. I felt like I could have helped her, but she hadn't given me a chance.

Despite everything that had happened, I still felt connected to Wren in some way. Maybe that would never die, just like my feelings for the French exchange student Mara had never really died. Even though I *was* over the moon about dating Carmelita. Maybe it was like that with everyone a person crushed on. Like the initial feelings still lived on, even though the person had moved on. Emotions couldn't be turned on or off like water in the faucet. It was one of my new ideas, but it intrigued me, and I'd have to see what else I came up with as time went on.

Will I had seen once or twice around school. He mostly kept to himself now from what we could tell.

"Look at this, Ziv," Carmelita called from the next bookshelf aisle.

I went over to find Car browsing through the store's New Releases section. She pointed to a newly released collection of Jack Kerouac's poetry, one that I didn't own.

"Wow," I said, picking the book up and leafing through it.

I thought back to all of Jack's work that I had been inspired by over the past few years. I thought back to his life philosophy that had always inspired me too. First thought, best thought. Living true to the self. Being honest.

One day I hoped to be published through City Lights Publishers. One day I hoped to come waltzing into the bookstore—after hanging around Caffe Trieste on Vallejo Street, after shooting the breeze with Bobcat at Vesuvio—and find my own book. I would autograph it on the fly and leave it for some Lit-nerd Henley student like me to find.

I walked over to the store's main display and stood in awe of the selected books that had been placed there: all of Kerouac's work, all of Ginsberg's work, Lawrence Ferlinghetti's too. The legacy of twentieth century San Franciscan writers, North Beach writers.

These writers had all written books that were genuine, that were true for them. It was the secret to their greatness, I was sure. Maybe that was why twenty-first century readers like myself loved them so much. They still held up.

"Just think," I said to Carmelita and Tyler, who

were on either side of me gazing at the display. "One day *we'll* be here. I mean, Car started it. First stop, lit journal contest. Next stop, published book. That's how it goes—and a bunch of concentrated work in between, of course."

"Of course," Tyler said with his arms folded across his chest and a mocking smile on his face.

"Hunter?" said Car. "You're getting too serious again."

"Right. Sorry," I agreed, putting my arm around her. "Fun first and foremost. For the future."

The three of us stood there in silence for a moment, daydreaming.

The future . . . or the future as it should be, I thought. Moving forward with good and reliable friends, who were seekers of truth and honesty and authenticity and fun. Who were works in progress.